Scandalist

Angela Evans

authorHOUSE®

AuthorHouse™
1663 Liberty Drive
Bloomington, IN 47403
www.authorhouse.com
Phone: 1-800-839-8640

Published by AuthorHouse 10/08/2014

ISBN: 978-1-4969-4630-0 (sc)
ISBN: 978-1-4969-4629-4 (e)

Library of Congress Control Number: 2014918171

Contents

Chapter 1

Lucy entered her apartment. She walked into the living room. Suddenly Lucy stopped, not being able to move any further. Lucy just stared as if an electric shock went through her body. As if someone had taken over Lucy moved quickly towards her live in boyfriend and began attacking him. He tried to hold her back and shield the blows. Ringing in his ear was, "Why would you do this?" She then turned her attention and began swinging at her son's girlfriend. Dressed in nothing more than crotchless lace panties Betsy managed to push Lucy off of her and began to run towards the door. Before she could get there, Betsy tripped over an end table that she and Paul had moved earlier. She fell hard missing her head on the television set. Lucy ran over to her and began hitting Betsy's head on the floor. Paul ran over to Lucy yelling for her to stop. Just as he reached Lucy, Bumper, Paul's son came in the front door. He heard the commotion and hurried into the living room.

"What's going on here? Momma what are you doing?"

Lucy screamed at the top of her lungs.

"This tramp was screwing your father."

Bumper looked at his father.

"Dad I don't believe you."

"You don't believe him? That's all you have to say?"

"Momma, I'm sorry."

"You're sorry. You don't have anything to do with this."

"I brought her here."

"You didn't tell your trampy girlfriend to jump on your father's…."

Lucy could not form the words. She pointed to Paul's private area.

Tears began to run down Lucy's face.

"Momma if I let you go will you go into your bedroom and be calm?"

"Bumper get them out of this house! No I'll leave."

Lucy jerked away from Bumper and walked towards her bedroom. She clumsily walked over to the closet. Flashes of the earlier scene went through her head. Lucy tiptoed trying not to touch much in the room. She opened the closet and took a large piece of luggage out. She began throwing clothes into the suitcase. Lucy ran around the room careful walking around the area where she thought they may have used. She walked around the bed as if there was something left from their encounter. Lucy closed the suitcase. She then proceeded to walk cautiously out of the room. Lucy stopped at the door when she heard talking.

"Dad I told you before you were going to get caught."

"I didn't know she was coming home early. She was supposed to be at work."

Lucy had to stop herself from entering the room. She wanted to hear the entire conversation.

"You shouldn't have been in the house."

"Man she usually work late."

"I told you one day she was going to bust you. You got my money?"

"I didn't finish."

"That's not my problem. If you had taken her to a motel, you would not be standing here busted up. You lucky you did not get killed. Betsy get up and get dressed."

"My clothes are in the bedroom."

"Well you're going to have to wait. Just sit down over there." Bumper pointed to the couch.

"I need to go to the hospital."

"Well because of mister stupid here you're going to have to wait until my mother leaves so you can get dressed and by the way dad you are going to have to give me three hundred more."

"What are you talking about? You said $200.00."

"That was before I had to take her for medical treatment."

"I only have $300.00. I cannot get anything from your momma now and my social security check is already spent. As a matter of fact I gave it all to you the last time."

"You only gave me $300.00."

"That's all I get?"

"What?"

"Yeah, your momma usually helps me out."

"Well that won't be happening any more. You're going to have to go get a $20 Hoe."

"You are going to do me like that?"

"It's nothing personal. This is business."

Lucy came into the room. The men stopped talking. She gave Paul a look that if looks could kill he would be ten feet under. Then she looked at Bumper. She could not believe she had raised someone else's child and treated him as her own and then he turned to do something like this. She then looked at Betsy. She was no longer angry with her, but pitied her for letting herself be used this way.

As Lucy walked out of the door without saying anything, she thought about herself. Lucy thought of how many years she and Paul had been together. She had met Paul at work when he was applying for social security for his son. He explained how his wife, Paul Jr.'s mother had deserted them. Paul said that he did not know how to take care of a little baby. Her heart had gone out to him.

Lucy stopped at the light. Lucy thought of how she offered to show him how to bathe and change the baby. One thing led to another and they were going out as a trio. After a few months, they moved in together. He was so loving. She could not understand why a woman would leave him. She thought of the way he expertly knew how and where to touch her. Lucy became aroused. She scolded herself. She heard a car horn beep at her. Lucy looked up and saw the light had changed. She continued on.

Lucy had driven for an hour before realizing that she did not have a destination. She saw a gas station and pulled into it. Lucy looked at the gas rang and then pulled along side of a gas tank. A man walked up to her car. She told the attendant to fill her tank up.

While the gas was being pumped into her car, Lucy began crying. She placed her head down on the steering wheel. The horn went off. The attendant stopped washing her front window and then came over to the driver side window. He asked her if she was all right. Lucy blurted out, "I have nowhere to go!"

"If you have some money there's a hotel about a mile down the street. It is a nice hotel. It is not a sleazy hotel. You look like a classy lady."

Lucy just wiped her eyes.

There was a click. The attendant glanced at the gas tank. He removed the nasal.

"That will be $47.00."

Lucy paid the attendant. He thanked her and she pulled off.

As she drove down the street, Lucy saw the neon sign up ahead. She pulled into the hotel's parking lot. Lucy parked the car, but did not get out. She was so tired. Lucy could not cry anymore. She felt empty inside…………………………………….............

After a while, Lucy heard a tap on the window. She looked up.

"Excuse me miss."

Lucy rolled her window down.

"Yes."

After seeing her distressed, he softened his tone.

"Are you alright?"

Lucy stared at the man. She did not know how to answer. Lucy asked herself, "Am I alright? What am I doing here? What am I going to do?"

"Miss is it someone I can call?"

Lucy continued to stare at him.

"Miss."

"I don't have anywhere or anybody."

"I don't believe that. I know there's someone."

"Believe it mister. I walked in on my live in boyfriend having sex with my stepson's what I thought was his girlfriend, well I guess since we never married he's really not my son. You know she was his prostitute slash girlfriend. I found out that all these years my boyfriend was using my money, (she patted her chest) to pay for a hooker. A hooker that the child I helped raise owned. Do you know I did all kinds of things to make sure this man was fulfilled? The jokes on me. I guess I didn't do enough."

"I think you probably did your best. I'm sorry miss, but you can't stay here in the parking lot."

"I don't have any place to go."

"I'm sorry. You can rent a room. I can give you one for a low price tonight."

"Fine."

The man stepped back. Lucy grabbed her purse. She took the keys out the ignition and then opened the car door. She followed the man into the hotel. He instructed the receptionist to set up a nice room for Lucy. A few minutes later, the woman handed Lucy a key and told her room number. The woman asked Lucy if she needed help with her bags. In a low tone, Lucy told her no. Lucy thanked the woman and then turned to the man and he nodded his head. Lucy walked slowly to the elevator. She pushed the up button. When the elevator opened there was a couple locked in each other's arms kissing. They did not move, so Lucy entered. She pushed the fifth floor button. Just as the doors were about to close the couple realized that, their elevator had arrived at the main floor. They looked at Lucy and apologized. The man grabbed the door. They quickly exited the elevator. The door closed and the elevator began moving. When it arrived at the fifth floor, the door opened. At first, Lucy stood still looking at the open door. Just as it was closing, she walked out of the door. Lucy looked down at her key and then up to figure out which way to go. Lucy began walking down the hall. When she reached her room, Lucy slid the key in the lock and then pushed the door open. Lucy allowed the door to close behind her. She leaned back on the door. A knock on the door startled her. She opened the door. It was the man from the parking lot.

"I just came up to see if you were alright."

"Thank you again for your assistance."

"No problem. Would you like some company?"

Lucy just stared at him. She did not know what to make of him. After a few minute, she moved back. The man walked in. He closed the door behind him. The man took Lucy's hand and guided her to the sitting area.

"I don't know if I introduced myself. My name is Reggie. It is short for Reginald Brown. I am the night manager of this establishment. I picked up your name Ms. Bridges."

Lucy looked up at him.

"Please call me Lucy."

"It would be my pleasure."

She looked at him curious wondering "Could this man be flirting with me?"

"I don't mean to step out of line, but you should not be crying over any man. You are too beautiful." Reggie placed his hand under he chin. Tears began to flow down her face.

"May I?" Lucy lightly nodded. Lucy thought he was going to wipe her eyes. She was surprised when he brought his face closer to hers and lightly kissed both of her eyes, slowly and gently. "If I could be forward would you like to be held?" Lucy just stared at him. Reggie positioned his chair in front of Lucy. He moved close to her. He placed his arm around her bringing Lucy closer to him. He moved her closer until he had both his arms around her. Lucy reluctantly laid her head on his shoulder. Although Lucy did not know this man, she needed comforting. Reggie caressed her back. When he felt her relax Reggie kissed Lucy on her neck. She did not move. Reggie pulled her closer. Lucy began to cry. Her body shook with grief. Reggie kissed her neck again and continued to caress her back. Then he moved back and looked into her face. Her head was still positioned on his shoulder. With a closed mouth, he kissed her on the lips. She did not move. He ventured further. Reggie parted her lips with his tongue. At first, he could feel that she was not into it. He stopped kissing her and asked if she wanted him to stop. Lucy did not speak. She shook her head no. Reggie smoothed his hand down the side of Lucy's face. She leaned her head towards it.

"You are a beautiful woman. You should never be sad." Reggie thought, "How can such a beautiful woman be so unhappy." He wanted to erase her sadness.

Reggie stood up. He held his hand out. Lucy took it. She was numb. Lucy allowed him to lead her to the bed. He sat down and she in turn followed his move. They sat next to each other. Reggie asked Lucy if she was all right. She being distraught with tear drenched eyes shook her head yes. Reggie got on his knees in front of her. He held her face in his hands. He kissed her eyelids, the tip of her nose and lightly on her lips. Reggie asked her to let him make the sorrow go away. At first Lucy stared at him in disbelief. Reggie was patient. She saw the kindness in his eyes. Lucy thought to herself, "Should I be here with this man, letting him kiss me and touch me as if we are a couple?"

Reggie broke her concentration. "Would you like me to leave?"

Lucy thought about the question. She just wanted to stop the pain.

As if he had read her mind, "Let me make the pain go away."

After a few minutes Lucy decided to submit. She laid back. Reggie remained on his knees. He was a large man, six foot three. She did not move. He caressed her body. Lucy tried not to cry, but could not hold them back. This did not stop Reggie's advances. He could tell that Lucy's body responded the way he wanted it to. Throughout his seduction, Reggie talked to Lucy. He told her all the things that would make a woman feel wanted. When he had completed his mission in bringing her body to the brink of calling out for completion he undressed. He laid beside her. Reggie kissed Lucy passionately. She forgot her troubles, wrapped her arms around his muscular neck and submitted to the passion. Lucy wanted to forget. Her body felt good and she wanted this feeling to last. Reggie removed her clothes. He stopped once for a second to prepare himself. Lucy welcomed him. She welcomed this feeling. She held onto this strong handsome man. He kissed and caressed her body making her mind whirl. Reggie brought her to a height that she longed for. She collapsed in his arms. Reggie kissed her passionately sealing their lovemaking. He held her for a few minutes. Then he asked if she wanted him to stay with her. Although she longed for him to continue holding her Lucy managed to assure him that she would be all right. She knew or figured he was on the job and should get back to his station. Reggie kissed her again and told her that she was wonderful. He got out of bed. As he gathered his things and went into the bathroom, she watched him. She wondered if she had been the first woman, he had come to rescue, to make feel better after a breakup. She wondered if his concern was just an act. Lucy feeling exhausted closed her eyes.

After   a   few   minutes   she   drifted   off   to sleep.......................................

When Reggie came out of the bathroom, he noticed that she had fallen asleep. He left his card on the nightstand. Reggie quietly left the room. He made his rounds......................

Chapter 2

The next morning after checking in with the desk clerk Reggie went to the restaurant. He ordered several items for breakfast. It was placed in a bag. Reggie went to Lucy's room and knocked on the door. There was not a response. He knocked again. A few minutes later, the door opened. Lucy peeped out. With a broad smile, showing beautiful white perfect teeth Reggie said good morning. He asked if he could come in. Lucy reluctantly moved back. Reggie explained that he was just checking on her and wanted to make sure she kept up her strength. Lucy not realizing her nakedness just moved back. Reggie could not help becoming aroused. He tried to turn his attention to something else. Reggie took the food out of the bags and placed it onto the table. He pointed to it and then asked if she wanted company. As if a statue Lucy continued to stand frozen. She did not know what she wanted. Lucy hurt from within. Reggie walked over to her. He engulfed her into his arms. She snuggled into his arms. His warm body and strength made her feel secure. Reggie picked her up and carried her over to the bed. He placed her onto the bed and then laid next to her. Reggie held her close to him and caressed her hair and shoulder. Lucy with tear soaked eyes fell asleep.

When Reggie felt Lucy's body relax, he eased her off of him and left the room. He made sure the door was locked. Reggie went to his office and completed some paperwork. A few times, he caught himself thinking of Lucy. His thoughts flashed to their night together. Then he thought of how close he was to her before leaving her room. He tried to stay focus, but could not stop thinking of her. Reggie thought of how he would like to have a relationship with Lucy, but knew she was not ready to get involved again. Reggie returned to her door in the evening. He knocked on the door, but did not get any answer...................

The next day before leaving Reggie returned to the door, but again there was not any answer. He left a note for the covering staff to call him if Lucy asked for him.

Two days later Lucy awakened and got out of bed. She dragged herself into the bathroom and showered. The warmth of the water was welcomed. She let the water run from head to toe. She washed her hair and smoothed soap over her body. An hour passed before she turned the water off and got out of the shower. She heard a knock on the door. Reggie flashed in her mind. She wrapped a towel around herself. Lucy opened the door. There was a stocky older woman standing there. The woman asked if she wanted her room cleaned. Lucy told her to come in. The older woman looked at the old food. She threw it out first. She looked at Lucy who had balled up in a chair. The woman asked if she was all right. Lucy nodded that she was. The woman asked if she was hungry. Lucy could not recall when she had last eaten, but she was not hungry. All she could think of was sleeping. Lucy balled up more and closed her eyes. The woman's heart went out to her. She cleaned up the room.

After making the bed, the woman let the covers back. After the housekeeper left Lucy got back into bed. She curled up and clutched a pillow. She fell asleep. A few times, she got up to go to the bathroom. She was sick. Friday she decided to go to the doctor. She called the doctor's office. Lucy was able to get an appointment. She was weak. Lucy was hungry. Before going to the doctor, Lucy stopped at a fast food place and got a breakfast sandwich. She ate a small amount and immediately had to pull over and throw up. When she had finished throwing up Lucy began driving again …………………………...............

When she arrived at the doctor's office Lucy parked her car. She was light headed so Lucy walked slowly. Lucy checked in. As she waited to be call, Lucy looked through the pages of a family magazine. She looked at the seemingly happy couples and their children. She thought of the day she arrived home early. Lucy was so happy and had a surprise to tell Paul. She had just discovered that she was pregnant. She was going to tell him that night. Now the thrill of it had gone.

When the nurse called her in Lucy knew what she had to do. When they entered the examining room, the nurse took Lucy's vitals.

Soon after the doctor came into the room, he asked Lucy how she was doing. Lucy explained that she was not feeling well. The doctor examined her and then told Lucy that everything was normal. Lucy told the doctor that she had decided not to have the baby. He questioned her and offered alternatives. Lucy asked the doctor to perform the procedure. Before conducting it, he asked if she was sure. Lucy told him that she was sure. She explained that it was something that she had to do. The doctor told her to undress.

When he returned, the doctor told her to lay back. He adjusted the table. He put Lucy to sleep. The doctor gave instructions to the nurse.

When he was done, Lucy was awakened. When she awakened, the doctor placed his hand on her shoulder and told her to rest. The nurse cleaned her up. After the nurse left the room, Lucy rolled onto her side. She was in pain. Lucy laid there for a while. The nurse checked in on Lucy a couple of times. Finally, Lucy drew up enough strength and eased off the table. Lucy slowly and painfully put her clothes on. When she had gotten dressed, Lucy left the room and headed to the front of the office. The nurse saw her and handed Lucy a prescription. She made an appointment to return. Lucy placed it in her pocket and left the office. Lucy slowly walked to her car. She got in it. Lucy sat for a few minutes. She was tired, lightheaded, and dizzy and in pain.........

After a few minutes, Lucy managed to turn the car on. She drove off.

As she drove off Lucy felt nauseated. She drove to the pharmacy. Although she hated to leave the car, she managed to ease out of the car and go into the store. Lucy ordered the prescription. She leaned over the seat in the pharmacy as they filled her prescription.

When it was done, she immediately took the painkiller. Lucy drove back to the hotel. When she pulled into the lot Lucy managed to park, but she could not move. She placed her head on the steering wheel...

A half hour later, she heard a tap on the window. Lucy managed to look up. It was Reggie. He could see something was wrong. He asked her if she could unlock the car. She slowly moved back. Shortly afterwards she unlocked the door. Reggie eased the door open. He reached in and turned the car off. He instructed Lucy to place her arms around his neck. She managed to do this. Reggie lifted her into his arms. She held him around his neck and rested her head on his chest. He held her close. Reggie took her through a side door to keep others from seeing her. He took Lucy up to her room. He used his master key to get in. Reggie closed the door behind himself. He gently laid Lucy in the bed. He asked if there was anything that he could get her. Reggie told Lucy that he would be back. Reggie went down to the restaurant and ordered some soup and a sandwich.......................

Reggie returned to Lucy's room. He knocked on the door. When there was not any answer, he opened the door with his swipe card again. Reggie walked over to the bed. Lucy was trembling. He eased her up. Reggie coached Lucy to drink some of the broth. She managed to drink half of it. He asked her what was wrong with her. Lucy managed to tell him what she had done. He asked if she needed something for the pain. She told him that she had already taken something. Reggie asked if he could see the medication. Lucy managed to point to her purse. Reggie went into it and retrieved the medicine. He read the pharmacy's warning and directions. He reached for the bottle of water that he bought upstairs, took a pain pill from the bottle and gave it to Lucy. She took it and then laid back down. Reggie caressed her hair for a while. He then left the room.............................

Two hours passed Lucy got up to go to the bathroom. She felt a little better. Lucy saw the sandwich on the nightstand. She ate half of it and then laid back down.

She awakened several hours later and took more medicine. Lucy felt better that night. She went down to the gift store and bought sanitary napkins. When she went back up to her room Lucy turned on the television. She flicked through the channels not actually looking at anything. As she channel surfed, a show caught her attention. It was of a woman giving birth. She watched intently until the baby had been born. Tears filled her eyes. She turned the channel..............

As the days went by Lucy began to feel better. She called work on Monday and told them that she would be out another week. After Lucy hung up the phone, she sat in a chair by the window. She looked out by the pool. A few people were lounging around the pool. She watched as a couple played in the pool. Another sat in the Jacuzzi. Lucy thought about her life. She had never gone on a vacation before. Lucy thought how she had helped to raise another woman's child. It had not been easy especially since she was only eighteen years old when she met Paul. She cared for his son as if he was her own. As he got older, Paul told Bumper that she was not his mother. From that moment on Lucy could feel the difference in the way Paul Junior treated her. She tried to remember Paul Junior and Betsy's relationship. "Did they ever act like a couple?" She thought they had, but to her dismay, it was a facade.

Lucy leaned back in the chair. She closed her eyes. Lucy began regretting the past twenty years. She had lived with a man, who she thought loved her. She had raised his son, who like his father had betrayed her trust and compromised her dignity. She was tired in her mind and body...

Lucy decided to remain at the hotel for a little while. She ran into Reggie on occasion and often thanked him for his kindness. On those occasions when she would see him, Lucy often wondered if she would have gotten through what she had if he had not assisted her. She also wondered if he cared for her out of pity. Everyday Lucy went into work as if nothing had changed in her life. It felt strange to be coming home to a hotel.

Two months passed and Lucy began looking for an apartment.

The day she moved out of the hotel Lucy thanked the staff for their kindness. Reggie was not at work so she left a note for him. She left a sizable tip for housekeeping. Lucy headed to her new place. She was happy to have more than one room. When she went up to her apartment, Lucy looked around. She did not have any furniture. Lucy was content that she had a place of her own. Lucy sat on the radiator and tried to figure out how she was going to get furniture. Her credit was not the best due to helping Paul. Looking out of the window Lucy saw a Rent-A-Center (RAC), truck pull up in front of her building. That gave her an idea.

Lucy left her apartment and drove to the nearest RAC. When she arrived there, the manager trying to come onto her promised that he could get what she wanted delivered the same day. Lucy looked around the store. She found a bedroom, living room and kitchen set. The manager gave her a discount on the furniture and a free week. The manager hinted at his coming over to dinner. Lucy thanked him for his help and left. As she was walking out of the store, she could feel him watching her. She got into her car and drove off. Before returning to her apartment, she stopped at the store to purchase cleaning supplies and food.

When she arrived home, a RAC truck was parked in front of her building. She got out of her car. When she walked up to the building, she heard her name being called. She turned. Standing in front of the truck was the manager. He smiled broadly. The manager walked up to her.

"Hi, I understand a beautiful woman needs some furniture. I thought I'd come by and make sure she gets everything she need."

"Thanks so much."

Lucy led the men up to her apartment. They helped carry her grocery and items she had rented. When they had placed the last item down all the men left except the manager. He asked if there was anything else, he could do for her. Lucy thanked the manager and told him no. He again expressed his interest and then left. Lucy closed and then locked the door behind him. She then began to arranged her furniture. When she was done, Lucy stood back and looked at her living room and then her bedroom. Lucy went into her kitchen and prepared dinner. When the meal was done, Lucy fixed herself a plate and sat down at the table. She said grace and then began to eat. As she ate, Lucy thought of how different it felt to eat alone. She had eaten alone many times, but not in her own place, not with no prospects of anyone coming in. Lucy finished eating and commenced to cleaning her kitchen. When she was done, Lucy went to bed. It felt strange being alone in this large apartment. She was exhausted so it did not take too long before she fell asleep...........................

Chapter 3

Lucy fell into the swing of things with her new life. She got up everyday went to work and returned home. Lucy kept to herself. She was always a private person, which made it possible for her to move on without anyone noticing anything different about her.........

Several months later Lucy was called up to the front reception desk. As she walked towards the receptionist to her surprise, Paul was standing at the window. Not sure if he was there for her Lucy tried not to look in his direction. She walked up to the receptionist. When the receptionist noticed her, she informed Lucy that Paul was there to see her. Lucy thanked her and then walked out into the waiting area. She motioned to Paul for him to follow her outside. They walked to a secluded area. Lucy could feel him watching her. When they had reached where Lucy thought was safe to speak, she asked Paul what he was doing there.

"Girl you look good." He tried to touch her. Lucy moved back. She felt a tinge of want for this man. She hated that she actually wanted him to hold her.

"Stop! What are you doing here?"

"I came to bring you home." He reached for her arm. This time he was able to smooth his hand over her arm. Her body tingled at his touch.

"Paul stop! Besides you can't take me anywhere."

"Don't be like that. Girl I love you."

Lucy looked at him with contempt.

"Love?"

"Yes I love you. Come on she did not mean anything. That was sex. Look, I cannot help it. I tried doing things alone when you were at work. Then my boy walked in on me and said that I did not have to do that. He said that he had this girl and she would do all the things that I wanted. I told him that I could not do that. He said that it would be worst to keep doing what I did and besides I would be better with you."

"So it was all for me."

"Woman I'm just saying I can't help it and I've tried. It is like a drug, but there is no medicine for it. Come back I will not ever bring it in the house again. I promise."

"You're serious?"

"Of course."

"I can't do this. I can't be with someone who can't be monogamous."

"I can. I am not in any relationship with anyone. It's just; it's like me taking my medicine."

"I'm sorry Paul I can't do this. I would always think of you with other women when we're having sex."

"But that's the thing I'll just be with Betsy. It would just be to ease the pain that comes over me."

"Do you think that makes it any easier?"

"Please Sweetie I love you."

"I love you, but we can't work." Lucy began walking away. Paul grabbed her arm and pulled her to him. He went to kiss her and she turned away. "Paul I can't. Let me go."

"I love you."

"Then you will have to stop."

Paul released her and Lucy walked away. She went back into the building. After returning to her desk, Lucy put her head in her hand. Tears filled her eyes. She wiped them away. Lucy tried to work, but she could not concentrate. She thought about her conversation with Paul. Then she thought how he looked, smelled and his touch. She became aroused. Lucy scolded herself. She thought, "How can I love and still be turned on by this man. Paul is handsome and he always smelled so good." She looked up at the clock. It read 4:00. She gathered her things, turned off her computer and then left. Lucy got into her car and drove off. She began to feel good that she had not given in to Paul. She wondered if he would return to her job. Lucy told herself that she would have to stay strong.

When she arrived home, Lucy prepared dinner. She sat down and ate. Lucy looked around her kitchen. She began feeling lonely. She looked at the clock on the wall. It was 7:00. Lucy decided to call her friend Ruth. Just as she thought, Ruth and a few others were going to a club. Ruth told her that it was women's night. She offered to pick Lucy up. Lucy accepted and gave Ruth her new address...

When Ruth arrived, Lucy was ready. When Lucy got into the car, Ruth had already picked up the other women. Ruth asked what is with the new address. Lucy told her that she had broken up with her boyfriend.

"What that good looking man didn't put it down well?"

"No, that wasn't the problem. As a matter of fact that's all he wanted to do."

"What's wrong with that?"

"I wasn't enough."

"So he cheated."

"No he has an addiction to sex."

"Really? I need one of those."

"No. I'm serious that's all he thinks of."

"Wow. Well we are going to have a good time with the girls. It will be like old times. I miss you girl."

The women chatted throughout the ride and filled Lucy in on what had been happening in their lives. Lucy felt like a teenager again. It seemed as if time had somehow stopped for these women. Although they did look a little older and bodies had changed filled out but mentally they had not aged much. Lucy just listened. She thought their mouths had gotten dirtier...

An hour later, the group arrived at the club. Ruth parked the car. They exited the car and headed towards the door of the club. The door attendant flirted with them and then let them in. The women walked over to the bar. They ordered drinks. The women had a few drinks and then went out onto the dance floor. They danced a while...............................

Then two men came up to them and began dancing with them. One of the men seemed to be interested in Lucy. A few times, he turned his attention to her and said a few words while they danced. She thought that he had to be a few years younger than her. Lucy smiled when he told her his name and then asked for hers. Lucy told him her name. Another song played and Lucy decided to sit down. She thanked the young man and left the dance floor. The young man stayed on the dance floor. Lucy sat and watched her friends dance with the two guys.

After a half hour, she got up, went over to the bar, and ordered a drink. Lucy found herself enjoying this moment. She sipped on her drink and continued to watch the dance floor. She remained at the bar.

One of the women with them came over to the bar. She asked Lucy what she was drinking. Lucy told her that it was the "House Special." The woman whose name was Mary Jane asked for a sip. Lucy told her that she could have it and she would order another one.

Mary Jane asked if she was sure. Lucy gave the drink to Mary Jane. Mary Jane took the drink and sipped it.

"This is good. I am so thirsty."

"I see."

"Hey maybe we can get those guys to buy us drinks." She pointed over to the two men.

"I have money."

"Girl you have been out of commission a long time. That is not how it is done.

"How is it done?"

Just then, the two men came over and asked what they were drinking. Mary Jane told them. The men ordered rounds for the group and then themselves. The men talked with the women for a while and then excused themselves.

After they left May Jane said, "See girl. You have to start getting out more."

"Maybe I will."

A song played that Lucy liked. She grabbed Ruth's hand and pulled her onto the dance floor. They danced a few minutes and then the man who had danced with Lucy before named Jonathan came onto the dance floor. He began dancing with the two women. He paid more attention to Lucy. Jonathan talked to Lucy while they danced. Ruth decided to leave the two on the dance floor together.

Jonathan danced up on Lucy. She allowed him to place his arm around her waist while they danced. Lucy in turn placed her arm on his shoulders. They danced to a few songs................

At one point Jonathan asked Lucy if they could get some air. She agreed, the two left the dance floor and then walked out of the club. There were others outside. Jonathan placed his arm behind Lucy's back and led her to the side of the building. Jonathan was so close she breathed in his air. His cologne was intoxicating. As he talked to her Lucy's mind wondered. She found herself turned on by his good looks. Lucy thought he must be much younger than her. His body was obviously well taken care of because from what she could see was muscular and his voice was deep and smooth. She tried to concentrate on what he was saying, but found herself listening to his voice without really hearing what was coming out of his mouth. When she tuned back into what was being said Lucy heard Jonathan ask if they could leave and go somewhere that they could be alone. Lucy was feeling good and wanted to say yes, but she did not want her friends thinking badly of her. Lucy expressed that she could not leave her friends. Jonathan asked if they could meet somewhere after she was dropped off. Lucy thought about it, knowing that she would not be able to drive anywhere, because she had been drinking and not use to it. Lucy knew that it would be definitely unwise to try.

Jonathan moved closer to her and asked if he could kiss her. The way she was feeling Lucy smiled. Jonathan took this as a yes. He bent down and kissed her. He was so gentle. Lucy's mind whirled. She reached up and placed her arms around his neck, wanting to feel him closer. Jonathan pulled her close. She could feel his need to be closer. This further enticed her. Jonathan stopped abruptly. He whispered in her ear that he wanted to get closer to her. Although she did not know this man Lucy was feeling the effects of the alcohol and wanted him as much as he wanted her. He whispered again asking if it was possible that they go somewhere. Lucy took him by the hand. This time he followed her as she led him back into the club.

When they entered the club, Lucy excused herself. He did not know if she had turned him down and he should view this as a failed attempt or if he should be patient and wait for her return. He watched as she walked over to her friends. Lucy talked to her friends and asked for their advice. She did not disclose her desires. Lucy told her friends that Jonathan wanted to give her a ride and that she would like to get to know him better. Her friends coached her to go for it. Ruth exclaimed that if she did not go she would take him up on his offer. Lucy hugged the women. Jonathan noticed her walking back to him. She smiled giving him confidence. When she was close, enough for him to hear she said, "Let's go. Jonathan smiled and then put his hand behind her back. They walked to his car. She was impressed, while it was not new; it was not very old either. He walked her over to the passenger side door of his Mercedes Sports. Jonathan opened the door. Her head was cloudy from the alcohol, but she thought that he could not be married with children owning a two-seater. She relaxed in the soft leather seats. Lucy watched this six foot one young man walk to the driver's side. He was very handsome. Jonathan got into the car. He started it up. Before pulling off, he looked at Lucy and asked if she wanted to go to his condominium. Lucy shook her head yes. She was relieved that he did not ask to go to her apartment. Jonathan turned on music. Lucy relaxed and enjoyed the music. Jonathan drove a distance...................

After some time they finally came upon a community. Jonathan swiped his key card and the gate opened. He drove a quarter of a mile before pulling in front of a two-story building. They got out of the car. Jonathan placed his hand behind her back and they walked to the building. He used his swipe card again and allowed her to walk in first. They walked pass four doors and then stopped.

Jonathan used his swipe card and they entered the condominium. After he closed the door, Jonathan asked Lucy would she like a drink. She accepted. Jonathan made both of them a drink. They sat in his living room. Lucy looked around the room. Although she had not seen the entire apartment, she was impressed with how nice his place looked. He took a sip of his drink and then placed it on the coffee table. He moved closer to her. Jonathan asked if she was comfortable. Lucy nodded that she was. He looked into her eyes. She could see desire in his eyes. She became nervous. Lucy took a sip of her drink. Jonathan ran his finger across her lips. He then ran the back of his hand down her arm. Jonathan moved closer to her. He placed his arm around her shoulders. He leaned back and closed his eyes. Jonathan caressed her shoulders. It sent shivers throughout her body. He sat up. With his eyes, still close Jonathan kissed her neck. He ran his tongue down the back of her neck. Lucy moved away from him placing her half-full glass on the table. Jonathan lay across the couch behind her. She looked back at him. Jonathan pulled her to him. He kissed her.

As he kissed Lucy, Jonathan caressed her back. Jonathan guided her to lie on top of him. She could feel the hardness of his body. He squeezed her body to his. She found herself wanting this man. He began to undress her. When Lucy had been stripped down to her underwear, Jonathan moved her onto the side of him. He then stood up and began removing his clothes. Jonathan watched her as he removed each item of clothing. He smiled as the expression on Lucy's face showed that she was impressed with his body. He lay back on the couch next to her. He began kissing her again and as he caressed her body, the kiss became more intense. Jonathan whispered her name telling her how beautiful she was and how good she felt, making Lucy feel closer to him. Lucy and Jonathan spent the night bringing each other's bodies to heights they had not imagined...................

Afterwards they laid there holding onto each other drenched in sweat. They soon drifted off to sleep…………………..

The next morning Lucy awakened. She looked over and saw that she was lying in this man's arms. She thought back and recalled her night with him. Lucy felt sick and jumped up. Jonathan awakened. He asked her what was wrong. Lucy's expression gave him his answer. He got up and showed her to the bathroom. She got down on her knees as quickly as possible. She was in the bathroom so long Jonathan came to the door and asked if she was all right. By then Lucy had stopped throwing up, but she was now ashamed of her behavior. She sat next to the toilet with her head down between her legs. Lucy managed to say that she would be out shortly. Lucy began to pray. She asked God for courage to leave the bathroom…………..

After a few minutes, Lucy got to her feet. She turned on the water and sprinkled it onto her face. Lucy then rinsed her mouth out. She combed her hair with her fingers. Lucy looked at her naked body. She looked at the towels in the bathroom, but did not want to bother them. She figured they were just for show. Lucy wished that it were a full bathroom so she could take a shower. She placed her hand on the doorknob. She finally turned it. When she came out Lucy was relieved that he was not there. She went into the living room. Lucy began getting dressed. Jonathan came downstairs. He was handsomely dressed in a t-shirt and blue jeans. He smiled at her with such tenderness she was no longer nervous. He held out his hand to her and without reservation, she walked over to him. She took his hand. He led her down the opposite hall. When they made it to the end of the hall, there was a bedroom. They entered it. They continued walking where there was an adjoining bathroom. He showed her where the towels were and a new toothbrush and toothpaste. He bent down and lightly kissed her on the lips. Lucy was thankful for his kindness. Jonathan left her.

She turned on the shower and then got in. The water felt good against her skin. She put her face in the water. When Lucy finished washing her body and rinsing off she dried herself. She put her clothes on. Lucy left the bathroom and found her way back to the living room. Jonathan was sitting there. When he saw her, he stood up. He asked if she wanted to get something to eat. Lucy declined. She was not really in the mood to eat. She felt guilty. Lucy explained that she was not feeling well. She was partly telling the truth. Lucy had gotten the alcohol out of her system, but she still was not feeling a hundred percent.

She was quiet during the first half hour. Jonathan broke the silence. He began talking about their night together. Jonathan told her how he enjoyed her company and then said that he would like them to get to know each other. Lucy was surprised. On some level Lucy thought Jonathan was being a nice person and just trying to make her feel better about the situation. When they finally pulled up in front of her building Jonathan asked for her number. Although she did not think that he would use it Lucy gave it to him. He leaned over, kissed her likely on the lips, and then opened her door. Lucy said bye and then shut the door. She went into her building.

When she entered her apartment, Lucy changed her clothes. She went to lie down, but noticed the light flashing on her phone. She walked over to it. She dialed her voicemail. There was a message left by her friends. She could tell that they were calling on their way from the club. They sounded drunk. The women yelled into the phone that they hoped she had a good time and wished a better night with Jonathan. She erased the message. Lucy lay down and drifted off to sleep....

Chapter 4

The next two weeks Lucy worked and stayed home on the weekend. Her friends called asking her to go out, but she declined.

Ruth and the other women went to the club. It was women's night and the women arrived early to get in free. They first sat at the bar and ordered drinks. They spotted several seats at a table and then left the bar. The women sat and sipped on their drinks. A couple of hours later people began coming into the club. Constance spotted a handsome gentleman come into the club and decided to try to meet him. Constance told the women that she was going to the ladies' room. As she walked toward the man, he happened to look her way. She smiled at him. He returned her smile and stopped walking. She came closer. The gentleman spoke and asked if she would like a drink. Constance accepted and they walked to the bar together. He introduced himself as Paul. They had a few drinks together and shared a brief conversation. The man wrote something on a piece of paper and handed it to her. He thanked Constance for her company and stood up. He took her hand in his and lifted it to his lips. The man kissed it and told her that he hoped to see her again. Constance asked him if he was leaving so soon. The man asked why. Constance told him that she would miss him. He looked at her curiously and then asked if she would like to go somewhere. Constance told him that she was there with her friends. He told her that they could go to his car and talk or do something. As he turned to leave the club Constance followed him. Once they were out of the club the man walked over to his car. Constance was interested in this man. He seemed so assure of himself. The man walked over to the passenger side of the car. He opened the back door. At first Constance just stared at the man. The man signaled for her to get in. After a few minutes Constance got in. The man followed her.

As Paul talked, he caressed her arm. Constance tried to concentrate on what he was saying. Her heart went out to him. He talked so lovingly about his ex-girlfriend. She could not believe that she had left him. Paul asked if he could kiss her. He looked into her eyes saying that he was so lonely. Constance allowed him to kiss her. She thought how he was such a good kisser. He caressed her body. Constance knew that she should not, but Paul was so handsome. After a little while things began getting more physical, she pulled away. Paul looked at her with his beautiful dreamy eyes. She told him that she could not go any further with him. Paul explained that it had been so long and he needed to be close to her. Constance told him that he could touch her, but they could not go any further. Paul kissed her again and then pulled her closer. Constance tried to stop him and then Paul told her that she was beautiful. He told her that he needed someone like her. Constance wanted to be that women. He took her clothes off. Constance figured she would let him see her body and maybe that would bring him relief without her going all the way. Paul caressed her body and then told her that he had to have her. Constance protested, but her words were lost. He kissed her passionate and continued his pursuit of getting relief. Constance continued to say no.

Paul joined them and began moving above her. Constance began to cry. Paul stopped and looked down at her. He kissed her tears and told her that he loved her. She looked up at him. He told her not to cry. He asked her to make love to him. Constance looked into his eyes. She told him that she could not do this. Paul looked down at their bodies and then said, "We're already here. If you move with me, it will feel better. I will make you feel good. I promise. Constance finally gave in. He did as he promised....................

After a while, Constance regained her composure. As she exited the car, Paul asked if she was going to call him. She said that she would. Constance returned to her friends who had not noticed her absence.

The women danced all night often stopping and getting more drinks. Constance often watched the door wondering if Paul would come back into the club. She didn't know why she wasn't angry with him. She didn't tell her friends and was withdrawn the rest of the night................................

After she arrived home, Constance looked at the note Paul had given to her. It had his name and phone number on it. Constance debated on whether to call him. She thought about their encounter. She was tired. Constance got ready for bed. She lay in bed wondering if she should be angry with Paul. Constance replayed the night in her mind, "Had he forced himself on her, or was it something she wanted?" She concluded that eventually she would have slept with him. Now she wondered what he would think of her now. Would he want to have a relationship with her?" She soon drifted off to sleep holding the note in her hand all night...................

A month went by and Lucy was feeling lonely. She called Ruth. She welcomed her company. This time Lucy decided to take her own car. She figured it would prevent her from over drinking. They set a time to meet at the club. Lucy arrived earlier and decided to go into the club. When she entered, Lucy looked around. A few women were there, but there weren't' any men. Lucy decided to get a drink. Lucy thought if she drank early enough she should be sober by the time the club closed................

By the time her friends arrived Lucy was on her third drink. The women stopped at the bar when they came in.

When the women spotted Lucy, they walked over to her. The women drilled her about Jonathan, but Lucy was closed lip. Realizing she was not going to divulge any secrets the women changed the subject. They talked of more carefree matters.............

As the club began filling up Lucy subconsciously looked for Jonathan. The women pulled her onto the dance floor. The women danced for hours. After some time Lucy left them on the dance floor and went back to the bar. She ordered a drink. As she reached for the drink a voice behind her asked if he would have a sip. She turned around. To her surprise and pleasure it was Jonathan. She was happy to see him and it showed. Ruth came up from behind her and took her drink. She sipped it. Jonathan asked what they were drinking. Lucy told him. With a charming smile Jonathan ordered another drink and sipped from it. He then handed it to Lucy. He paid for the drink and led her to an empty table.

"You know I've been looking for you to come here every weekend."

"Really?"

"You sound surprised."

"I didn't mean to. It's just you didn't call."

"Did you want me to?"

"I gave you my phone number."

"Yes you did, but I got the impression that you weren't as interested in getting to know me as I was in you."

"I don't usually do things like I did the night we met."

"I didn't think you did. I felt privileged."

Lucy looked at Jonathan suspiciously, making him smile.

"Oh you think I'm running a line? Truly I think you are a classy woman and I would like to get to know you if you would allow me to. Would you like to dance?"

"Sure."

"Finish your drink."

Lucy turned up the rest of her drink. Jonathan stood up. He held his hand out. Lucy took it. They walked onto the dance floor. He pulled her close and danced provocatively. They remained this way throughout the song.

When the next song played Lucy managed to pull herself away. She liked his touch, but she did not want to appear so easy. He gave her a seductive smile. Lucy turned around to keep from blushing. He went to dance up on her at the same time she turned around. Jonathan cupped Lucy's face and kissed her on the lips. She returned his affection. Lucy realized it was no need pretending anymore. She was attracted to this man and enjoyed his company. Lucy glanced over at her friends. She felt guilty that she was spending most of her time with Jonathan. Lucy expressed this to Jonathan. He bent down and whispered in her ear if they could meet up at his place. Without waiting for an answer he asked if she remembered how to get there. Lucy nodded yes. Jonathan mistook this as she was agreeing to meeting him, not that she was saying yes that she knew how to get to his house. He kissed her lightly and said that he would see her soon. She did not think about it until reaching the table where her friends were sitting. Ruth asked her if she was enjoying herself. She answered yes. Ruth then asked why she was at their table. Lucy told them that she felt guilty spending all of her time with Jonathan. Lucy's friends teased her first, making her feel worst. They laughed and told her do not be stupid and to go spend time with him. Lucy asked if they were sure. Ruth told her if she did not go she was crazy. Lucy thanked her friends for their understanding and then left their table.

Constance excused herself and left out of the club. She dialed the man's number that she had met on a previous visit to the club. The phone rang several times before he answered. When he did Constance told him who she was. She realized that he probably did not remember her. She refreshed his memory. He then appeared to recall giving her his phone number. She noticed something in his voice. Constance asked him if she had called him at a bad time. The man took a few minutes before answering her and then sounding out of breathe told Constance that her timing was perfect. He seemed preoccupied, but remained talking to her. Again he stopped talking. He seemed to be moving. Constance tried to press her ear closer to the phone to try to get a sense of what he was doing, but because of the noise from the club she was not sure of what she heard. The phone was then quiet, as if it had been placed on mute. Although it took a while for him to come back to the phone Constance remained holding on. She wondered several times if she should hang up, but something would not let her………..

A half hour later the man said hello. His voice was clear, different she thought. She sensed that his distraction was no longer there. He seemed to be smiling. The man asked what she was doing. She told him that she was at the club. The man asked if he could pick her up and they do something together. Constance was hesitant, but wanted to see the man. She remembered how handsome he was and very charming. Constance breathed in and then agreed. The man told her to be outside of the club in an hour. Constance said that she would and then they hung up. Constance was excited and nervous at the same time. She walked back inside of the club…………………..

Lucy surveyed the room. As she walked pass the dance floor. Lucy saw Jonathan dancing with a young woman. She thought that the woman looked about his age. Lucy thought the two looked like they would make a good couple. They appeared to be enjoying each other. Lucy watched them dance to a couple of songs………………..

As if feeling her watching him Jonathan looked over and saw her. He placed his hand on the woman's shoulder. Jonathan thanked the woman for the dance and excused himself. Lucy looked on as the woman watched him walk away. Lucy could see the disappointment in the woman's face. Jonathan came over to her.

"What's going on?"

"My friends thought I should be with you."

"Truly? They are smart women."

"I'm not taking you away from your friend there? She seems disappointed."

"Don't worry about that. It was only a dance. I was keeping busy while waiting for you."

Jonathan guided her to the bar. He ordered a round of drinks and sent them over to the women. When the drinks were delivered to them the woman looked over to the bar. They held the drinks up to him. Jonathan nodded his head in acknowledgment. Lucy and Jonathan remained together until the club closed. Jonathan walked Lucy to her car. He asked if she had thought about his offer. Not wanting to seem like that is all she thought about Lucy pretended that she did not remember their conversation. Jonathan refreshed her memory. She wanting nothing more than to be with this man asked how would they do this. Jonathan offered to follow her home and then drive to his place.

After a few minutes Lucy agreed. She waited until he pulled up. Lucy pulled off. Jonathan stayed close behind her. After she parked Lucy held her hand up for him to wait. She ran into her building…………………………………..

A half hour went by. Constance told her friends that she had met someone and the man was coming to pick her up. The women asked who the man was. Constance told them that he was a bit older than they were, but very handsome and charming. The women asked if they could meet him, but Constance fearing the man would be turned off told the women next time……………………….

When she entered the apartment Lucy grabbed personal items and placed them into her purse. She looked around the room trying to think of what else she needed. Lucy went into her closet and grabbed a pair of jeans. She went into her draw and got a top. Lucy ran into the bathroom, grabbed her toothbrush and toothpaste. She exited her apartment, locked the door and walked down the hallway. Lucy rushed down the hallway not wanting to keep Jonathan waiting any longer, but then she slowed down, for a brief moment she thought, "Should I be doing this? I do not know this man. I must be losing my mind."

Constance kissed her friends and told them that she would call them the next day. The women told her she better.

Constance left her friends and walked out of the club. She waited forty-five minutes passed the time Paul had given her. A few times she thought of going back inside of the club, but did not want her friends asking what happened. She finally saw a late model BMW pull up to her. The passenger side window opened. A man leaned over and spoke. After seeing his beautiful smile Constance's apprehension disappeared. She bent down and spoke. He told her to get in and Constance did as she was told. He unlocked the door and Constance got into the car. The man pulled off.........................

Lucy slowed down and thought of turning around. Then she thought, "I can't just leave him out there. I have to tell him that I can't go." She picked up her pace again. Lucy looked at Jonathan standing outside of his car waiting for her, watching her. By the time she had reached him Lucy forgot her thought of not going. There was something about the way he looked at her. It made her not want to be sensible. He walked over and opened the passenger door. She got in. He closed the door and walked back over to the driver side door. He got in and started the car. As he drove Jonathan told Lucy about himself. He told her that he was a pilot. He saw the surprised look on her face. He asked her why she had a surprised expression. Lucy explained that it was surprising that he was a pilot when he looked so young. Jonathan explained that he was indeed a pilot. Jonathan reached into his pocket and pulled out his wallet. Lucy looked at his picture and then could not resist looking at his date of birth. She discovered that he was not much younger than she was. Jonathan noticed and asked about her expression. Lucy explained. Jonathan smiled and said, "Oh you thought you were robbing the cradle. So are you not interested now?"

"Yes I am. I actually feel better now."

"Why is that?"

"I didn't want to be taking your youth away. I had that done to me, so I would not want to do that to anyone, but we are not talking about me. Please continue."

She listened intently. Lucy found herself liking this man. Lucy thought how she could listen to his voice all the time. When he asked her about her life she told him that it was not half as interesting as his. He insisted on her telling him. Lucy found herself telling Jonathan about her breakup with Paul. Jonathan caressed her arm feeling that the hurt was still fresh. He did not interrupt her. Jonathan wanted to know what he was up against. By the time she was done with what she called her tragic story they were pulling into his complex. Jonathan parked. He squeezed her hand and they got out of the car. They walked into his building hand in hand.

When they made it to his door he put the swipe card in the door. Jonathan opened the door for Lucy to go in. She walked in the door. Jonathan walked in afterwards. He closed the door behind them. Jonathan led her into the living room. Lucy sat down. He asked if she wanted a drink. Lucy declined. Jonathan sat next to her and placed his arm around her shoulders. He leaned over and kissed her. Lucy returned his kiss. She placed her hand on his muscular arm. Lucy caressed it as they kissed. Jonathan thought of the pain she went through. He wanted to make her forget. Jonathan caressed her body until she begged for him to complete her. Jonathan did not obey. He wanted them to take their time. He knew this woman was special. He could see himself with her. Jonathan held back until he too could not stand being apart from her any longer. Jonathan obeyed their bodies. He made them one. They started out wanting to savor the moment, but then their bodies took over. Their minds no longer in control. Jonathan lost himself. He found himself pulling her closer, squeezing Lucy's body, and then whispering in her ear he was falling in love with her. Their bodies relaxed and they fell asleep……………

After driving for an hour the man pulled up in front of a house. He parked and then turned the car off. The man got out of the car. Constance sat in the car a few minutes having second thoughts about getting out. She did not want the man getting the wrong idea. The man closed his door and walked towards the house. Constance could not believe what was happening. She remained in the car. The man walked up to his house and opened the door. He walked into the house leaving the door open. When he did not return to the car Constance got out and walked towards the door. When she got to the door Constance peered inside. She did not see anyone. Constance entered the house and closed the door behind herself. To her surprise the man came into the living room with two glasses and a bottle of Grey Goose. He smiled at her.

"So you decided to come in? I was hoping that you were as interested in me as I am in you."

Constance smiled thinking, "He does like me."

"Please sit."

The man held his hand towards the couch. Constance sat. She was nervous. Constance had never gone to any man's house before at least not before getting to know more than his name. With confidence he handed her one of the glasses and poured the liquid. After pouring some in his glass he put the bottle down and clicked her glass saying, "To us." He smiled and drank some of the liquid. Constance nervously sipped some of the liquid. The man knew she was nervous and reassured her that he was not going to harm her. He sipped on his drink again and then placed it on the table. He got up and walked towards the stereo. Constance watched him thinking how handsome he was. She admired his confidence. Paul turned on music. Constance was surprised that it was not slow.

The man turned around and then held his hand out.

"I know I took you away from your friends and party. Can I make it up to you? May I have this dance?"

Constance got up and walked over to him. He began to dance. She was surprised how good he danced and she liked how sexy he moved. The man danced up on her. She permitted it. They danced to a few fast songs and then a slow one came on. Paul placed his arms around her waist, not bothering to turn her to face him. He moved with perfection, bringing her to arousal. He kissed her neck. His warm breathe and cologne arousing her senses. She allowed him to move his hands up to her breast. They continued to dance. Another song came on. It was fast. To her surprise the man released her and began dancing at a faster pace. She went along with it.

Before the song had changed again the man stopped dancing. He took her hand and led her to sit on the couch. He handed Constance her drink.

He picked his up and sipped from it. He commented, "You are a good dancer. I like the way you move."

"You are very good yourself."

Constance was feeling more comfortable. She watched as the glass touched his lips. Constance thought his lips were sexy and recalled them on her neck.

He finished his glass and then poured more into his glass. Although she had not finished hers Paul poured more into her glass as well. She was thirsty from their dancing and drank more. Paul placed his glass down and leaned back onto the couch. He smiled, but not just any smile, it was sexy. He smoothed his finger along the side of her arm. Constance shivered. She became nervous again and sipped her drink.

"Can I get comfortable?"

Constance was not sure what he meant, but nodded her head in agreement. The man got up and left the room. Constance was happy for his control. Constance watched as he walked away, thinking how he even walked sexy.

He was gone a few minutes. Constance drank more of the liquid and took this time to look around the room. She thought how nice his house was. Constance thought it had a woman's touch. She looked for pictures to tell her if he was single. There were none and she presumed that maybe a woman had lived there once. She was almost sure there was not one now. Constance finished her drink and placed it down onto the table.

The man returned. He had taken his dress pants off and put on shorts. She could not help notice the print in the front. She tried to look away. The man noticed and smiled. She did not see him notice. He sat next to her. Paul poured more liquid into her glass and then handed it to her. She accepted it and sipped from it.

Paul then asked, "May I?" He leaned closer to her and she allowed him to kiss her lips. He commented, "Sweet."

He took the glass out of her hand and put it to her lips. She drank from it. He in turn drank from the same glass. He leaned in again and kissed her. The man repeated this until they had finished the bottle.

Paul placed the glass down. He kissed her leaning into Constance until she moved against the back of the couch. He asked if she was comfortable. She said that she was, but he adjusted her body saying, "Isn't this better?"

Constance did not speak. The man began kissing her again. Constance thought how good a kisser he was. She was surprised that he had not tried to touch more than her breast. Although she did not want to be seen as easy Constance wanted him to touch her like he had when they were dancing. She craved his touch. The man stopped kissing her and moved to her neck. He could tell that she was turned on. He resisted touching her body with his hands, which was torture, but Paul wanted to make sure that when he did she would be ready. They remained with him kissing her for some time..............

He knew she was ready when Constance placed her arms around his shoulders and squeezed them. He placed his arms under her legs and lifted her into his arms. He remained seated and pulled her closer to him.

After some time Paul stood up with her in his arms and carried her into his bedroom. When Paul entered the room he walked over to his bed. He stopped and looked into her eyes. He asked, "Are you ready?"

Constance wanted him. She hated that it was so soon and it showed.

"Don't worry about it. I know you are not easy. There is something here. I want you." He laid her onto his bed. Paul laid next to her. "I will feel the same way that I do tomorrow as I do today. Let yourself feel what's happening here." He took his hands and ran his fingertips down her arms. He kissed her neck and then placed his hand under her chin. He looked at her so tenderly that Constance knew she could not deny him what he asked. She placed her arms around his neck and they were lost....................

The next morning Lucy awakened first. She looked around and realized where she was. Lucy laid there with her head on Jonathan's chest. She thought about their conversation. Then she remembered their lovemaking and the way he touched her and the way it made her feel. All of a sudden Lucy thought of his whisper. She wondered if what he had said was from the heat of the moment. Lucy wondered could he really have more than lustful feelings for her.

She snuggled up to him, loving the smell of his body and its masculinity. She nestled her face in his chest. Lucy thought how she could get use to being in his arms. She told herself to stop. "How can I be thinking these things about a guy I barely know?" Jonathan stirred. He held her tighter. He then reached for her face. Jonathan pulled it up to his and kissed her passionately. At first Lucy kept her mouth closed. After several attempts of Jonathan trying to kiss her with an open mouth Lucy gave in. She had never kissed anyone before brushing her teeth. After a while Lucy was lost in his passion……………..

Constance woke up. She looked over at the man. He was still asleep. She eased out from underneath him. Constance eased out of bed. She stopped at first feeling pain. She slowly walked over to the bathroom and closed the door. She looked at herself. Constance could not believe what they had done the night before. She had never done such things. She could not believe how often they had sex either. She had never known a man to have so much stamina and be ready to have sex again so quickly. She heard a knock on the door and then the door opened. He walked over to her and began kissing her. He picked her up, carried her into the bedroom, and placed her onto the bed. Although she was very sore Constance did not say no. The man noticed and got up. He retrieved some ointment and placed it on her body, messaging it. Constance was taken with this act of kindness. Thinking how thoughtful he was she ignored the pain and went along with his desire……………

When he finally stopped to rest Constance whispered that she needed to get home. The man moved off of her and looked at Constance.

"Stay with me." Constance looked at him confused. "You heard right. I need you. I want to be with you. You are so gorgeous. You can live here with me and we can be together."

Constance could not believe what she was hearing. No man had ever expressed anything remotely as having a relationship after they had made love.

"I'm not sure of what you're saying."

"I'm saying that I need you here with me. Always."

"Paul are you sure?"

He kissed her passionately. He held her in such a desperate way that Constance felt incline to grant him his wish. They stayed in bed the rest of the weekend...................

Several hours later Jonathan awakened. Lucy was still asleep. He got up. He went upstairs and showered. When he returned downstairs Lucy was awake. He smiled and said, "You know where the bathroom is."

Lucy picked up her purse and headed down the hall.

When she entered the bathroom Lucy turned on the water. She stepped into the shower and washed herself.

When she was done Lucy grabbed a towel and dried off. Lucy put on a pair of shorts and a t-shirt. She put on deodorant, lotion and sprayed perfume over her body. Lucy left the bathroom and headed down the hallway. She heard something. Lucy did not want to be nosey, but her curiosity got the better of her. Lucy called out. After a few minutes Jonathan came downstairs. He held his hand out. Lucy took it. He walked backwards staring at her. He climbed up the stairs backwards, keeping his eyes on her.

When they entered the room Jonathan asked her if she liked the room. Lucy told him that it was a nice bedroom. He asked her if it was nice enough to move in. Lucy looked at him curiously.

"I would like you to move in here." Lucy continued to stare at him, not believing what she was hearing. "I don't usually move this fast, but I care for you. If it's too soon I can wait."

"I need time."

"No rush. I don't normally bring women here." Lucy looked at him unbelieving. "Really I have brought a few women that I really liked to my place, but they have never made it up here."

"So I'm special."

"Don't say it like that. I saw that you were different."

"How?"

"You're pure."

"Pure?"

Jonathan smiled.

"I don't mean it in that sense completely. Your heart is pure. You could not have taken care of another woman's child if you weren't a good person. I can see a future with you."

"You don't know me."

"I know enough, but if you give us a chance we can get to know each other better."

"I thought that's what we were doing."

"You can't hold back. No reservations okay?"

"I'll try my best."

Jonathan placed his arm around her back and led her out of the room and downstairs.

"So do you have any plans today? Can we get started getting to know each other?"

"No, I don't have any plans."

"Do you like the beach?"

"Yes."

"Are you hungry?"

"A little."

"We can get something on the way."

"Where are we going?"

"The Beach."

Jonathan and Lucy left his condominium...........................

After getting something to eat the couple got on their way. Lucy was happy that they made light conversation. Lucy did not know how she felt about a serious relationship. Lucy had been in what she thought one and found out she was being used. Lucy had given up her youth and never once thought she would have to begin a new life with someone else. Lucy thought of all the years waiting for Paul to legalize their relationship and was ecstatic when she discovered her pregnancy, only to come home................

A tear dropped down her face. Lucy sniffled. She tried to wipe the tear away without Jonathan noticing.

"Are you alright?"

Lucy tried to clear her throat, to shield her emotions.

"I'm fine."

Jonathan glanced at her and at the same time took his hand to turn her face to see better.

"Are you thinking about your ex?"

"I'm sorry. I did not mean to. I was thinking about what you asked me this morning and it made me think of him."

"Don't worry about it. I just have to try harder to make you happy."

"Jonathan it's honorable that you want to make me happy, but it's not your responsibility. This is on me. This is something that I have to work through and I will. I promise this will not be your burden and I will try not to get like this around you."

"That may be difficult, because I plan to spend as much time with you as I'm allowed." Lucy looked at him. "Don't worry about it."

Lucy changed the subject and began talking about the scenery.

A half hour later they arrived at the beach. Jonathan parked. He asked her if she wanted to walk on the boardwalk or go onto the beach. Lucy chose the boardwalk, because she did not have a bathing suit with her. Jonathan looked at her with his beautiful eyes. It felt nice. She had never done this before. Lucy turned her attention and was amazed when she saw a woman with a cart full of plates feeding the homeless. She watched a few minutes, observing how grateful they were and how the people seemed to know her. Lucy expressed to Jonathan that she thought the woman had to be a good person to do this. Jonathan told Lucy that the woman's name was Mary and that he had talked to her about it once. Lucy was surprised.

Jonathan explained that he used to spend a lot of time at the beach and that he became curious of the woman when people surrounded her every time she came onto the boardwalk, even when she did not have any food. Jonathan told Lucy that he had become curious, so whenever he came down to the beach he looked on. One day he was walking along the boardwalk and she was handing out food. He walked up to her. She offered him a plate. Jonathan was hesitant, but accepted it, because he did not want the homeless to think anything was wrong with it. He thanked her and moved on. When he got out of site he handed the meal to a family digging in the garbage...........
Jonathan placed his arm around her shoulders, bent down, and kissed Lucy on the forehead. He asked if she was hungry. Lucy shook her head yes. Jonathan led Lucy to a restaurant not far down the boardwalk. They entered the restaurant and were immediately seated. Lucy looked around the restaurant. She thought it beautiful. It was partly full. She noticed a lot of couples and some families. Lucy thought of Jonathan's question about moving in with him. She looked at him. Lucy could see herself with this man, but resolved that she needed more. Living with him would not be enough. She had done that and what had it gotten her. No it would have to be marriage or nothing. Jonathan noticed she was in deep thought.

"Penny for your thoughts."

Lucy smiled at his statement. She apologized. Jonathan asked her if everything was alright..............

The waitress walked up to their table. She asked them if they wanted to order anything to drink. Lucy looked at the drinks menu and ordered. Jonathan told the waitress that he would have the same. Lucy told the waitress, still looking at Jonathan, that she was ready to order. The waitress took out a pad and wrote down their order.

While they waited for the waitress to return Lucy commented on the restaurant. Jonathan did not pursue his earlier question. They made light conversation throughout their time in the restaurant............

When they were finished eating the couple decided to go to a club. Lucy purchased an outfit and put it on in the dressing room. Lucy liked the way Jonathan looked at her when she came out of the dressing room. He held his arm out. She put her arm in his and they left the store. They returned to his car and Jonathan drove to the club. He parked in one of the casino's hotels. They walked down to the club.

When the couple entered the club they were welcomed and seated. It was early so the couple had a few drinks.

When the club began to fill up Jonathan asked Lucy to dance. She stood up and they began to dance. Although the music playing was fast, Jonathan held Lucy close. They stayed on the dance floor most of the night, only stopping twice to have drinks....... When the club closed Jonathan asked Lucy if she mind them staying until morning. Lucy was thrilled, but did not want to show it. She had never been to Atlantic City before. She agreed immediately...................

Lucy stood next to Jonathan as he checked in. He asked if she was ready to go up to their room. She asked if they could go into the casino. Jonathan said yes. He showed her how to play some of the table games. They also played the slots a while. Just as they were about to leave Jonathan hit. They waited for the attendant to come over…………..

When the attendant arrived Lucy was surprised to find out that Jonathan had won five million dollars. Lucy could not believe it and even more how claim he was. Two men came over, asked for his identification and then gave him his check. His room was upgraded to a presidential suite.

When they got up to their room Lucy was excited. She looked through the suite, this time showing her excitement. Jonathan walked up to her and took her into his arms. He began kissing her. Lucy lost herself in his passion……………..

As they lay in bed Jonathan caressed her shoulders. He then smoothed her face with his and to her surprise he asked, "Marry me."

For a few seconds she laid quiet, not believing she heard him correctly. He whispered it again. Caught in his trans and the romance of the day Lucy answered in a low whisper, "Yes."

The two fell asleep……………...

The next day they both woke up simultaneously. Jonathan looked down at Lucy. He kissed her passionately. He then asked her was she ready? Lucy gave him a confused look. He looked at her, but did not speak. After a few minutes she remembered.

"You didn't mean immediately?"

"Not really, but why not?"

"There are things to do."

"You said you didn't have any family so there's no one to notify. There are shops in the hotel to get a dress for you and a tuxedo for me. I know they have to have a justice of the peace who would perform the ceremony."

"Jonathan."

Jonathan got on his knees and took her hand.

"I know this seems crazy, but I am in love with you. Marry me. Be my wife. I promise I will take care of you and I will be a good husband. I promise." He kissed her hands. Lucy just stared at him, not believing what he was asking. She looked into his eyes. What she saw in his eyes made her want to answer yes to all that he ask. After she answered him Jonathan picked up the hotel phone and called guest services.........

An hour later he and Lucy left the suite. They got into his car and drove around looking for a bridal store. They finally found one. Lucy refused to let him shop with her for the dress. She instructed him to meet her in an hour.

Lucy looked through many gowns and then found one..................

When she left the store Jonathan was waiting in the car outside of the store.

When Jonathan noticed her he got out and opened the back door. Lucy laid her dress across the seat. Jonathan noticed a travel agency and then asked Lucy where she would like to go on their honeymoon. Lucy looked at him stunned. She had not thought of that. He took out his cell phone and dialed a number. He was on the phone a little while. When they pulled back into the hotel parking deck Jonathan ended his call. He looked at Lucy and asked how she felt about going to Jamaica. Again stunned, Lucy could not speak. He explained that there was a flight at midnight. Lucy reached over and hugged Jonathan around his neck. "I guess you are in agreement."

"Are you kidding me? I'm just so surprised."

"Why?"

"Because no one has ever done anything like this before."

"Well stick with me." Lucy continued to hug him. "Sweetheart while I'm enjoying this we still have some things to do."

Lucy released him. They took their things out of the car. Jonathan checked in at the front desk. He was told that everything would take place at three that afternoon. Jonathan went down to the floor that they were scheduled to get married on.

Lucy called Ruth. Ruth thought she was joking at first. Once she accepted what Lucy told her Ruth told her that they were coming to give her support. Lucy asked if she would be her bridesmaid. Ruth was ecstatic…………..

Once Ruth hung up with Lucy she called the other friends.

Constance told Paul about her conversation with Ruth. She explained that she needed to get back to her place to meet her friend. Paul questioned her asking about these friends she was planning to go down the shore with and their plans. Constance named them and explained why they were going. She noticed the strange look Paul got when Lucy's name was mentioned. He asked for her last name, thinking that it could not be his Lucy. When Constance told him his expression changed. Constance questioned him and he confided that they had once dated. Constance remembered the conversation that she and her friends had when Lucy first went out with them.

It was Paul's turn to question Constance about her expression. She confided about the conversation. He sat up and then explained about his addiction. Constance was quiet for a while. Paul broke her concentration. He asked what she was thinking about. She looked away. Paul told her that he would always love her and if she truly loved him that she would stay with him. Paul told her that he would never love anyone the way that he loved her. She looked at him surprised. He placed his hand under her chin. He told her to look at him. She did as she was told. He looked at her with his beautiful big eyes and asked if she believed that he loved her. Again she looked away. He brought her face to his and kissed her passionately. While Constance could not believe he could love her she returned his passion.

After a few minutes Constance said that she had to leave to meet her friends. It was as if he did not hear her. He began caressing her body. She felt his need to be close, but they did not have much time. She expressed this. Paul stopped. He looked at her. Constance looked into his eyes. She did not recognize this look. It was as if he was someone else. His mind no longer ruled. Paul began kissing her again. She could sense him being out of control. He leaned her back. Although she knew they had to leave Constance went with his passion and sub-come to it.

An hour later they got up and dressed. He drove her back to her place. Constance got out of the car and ran into her house. Shortly after she heard a knock. She thinking it was her friends Constance ran to the door half dressed. She was mistaken. It was Paul. She noticed him look at her. She protested. He begged saying it would be quick and it would help him get through until she returned. Constance went with it.

When they were done she heard a horn blow. Constance jumped up and gathered her clothes. She kissed Paul and quickly left him. Constance ran and jumped into her friend's car. She spoke to everyone. Ruth asked what she had been doing. Constance told her that she was trying to find something to wear. Ruth accepted it. They prayed before getting on the highway. Ruth drove like she was taking a pregnant woman to deliver a baby to the hospital. During their drive Ruth asked Constance about the night she left the club. Constance told them that she had met a man. She explained that they were just getting to know each other. She was afraid to tell them that it was Lucy's ex-boyfriend……………..

Jonathan called his best friend and told him of the news. His friend thought he was joking and then after a few minutes of convincing his friend said, "Ah man, not you. I cannot believe it. Why is she pregnant?"

Jonathan assured him that it was not for that reason, but he did begin to wonder if she could be pregnant, since they had not used protection. Jonathan dismissed that thought to the air since they were about to get married. He smiled at the thought of how he would love to have children with Lucy.

"Hey man, are you there?"

"Yes. I was just in deep thought. So will you be my best man at three today?"

It was his friend Raymond's turn to be silent.

"Raymond, are you there?"

"Man I know you didn't just say you were getting married today."

"Yes I did."

"How long have you been dating this woman?"

"Man it's not about time."

"Man I don't believe you. I taught you better than this."

"Man I'm in love with this woman."

"Well she must be good. Are you sure it's not lust?"

"Are you coming or what?"

"Yes I'll be there. Where am I coming?"

Jonathan gave Raymond the name of the hotel and where to come. After getting off the phone he sat thinking about what he was about to do...................

As it got closer to the time he began getting nervous.

Back in the suite Lucy began getting dressed. She thought of how crazy it was of what they were about to do. She heard a knock on the door. Lucy stood behind the door and opened it slowly, hoping that it was not Jonathan. It was her friends. They burst in and hugged her. They made jokes about her being sprung. Then the women became serious. They looked at Lucy in her dress and told her that she looked beautiful. Constance did their make-up. The women had chosen matching colors...............

At two forty-five there was a knock on the door. Mary Jane went to open it. It was a staff person from the hotel. He explained that he was there to escort her to the chapel. He asked if she was ready. Lucy told him that she was. The group followed the man. They were taken to a holding room. In the room was the coordinator. She introduced herself as Karen. Karen greeted the women and then explained the arrangements..............

At three thirty the organist began playing music. The maid of honor and bridesmaids began to walk up to the front of the room. Jonathan was surprised. He was then taken aback when Lucy entered the room with a traditional wedding dress with a full veil. He watched as she came closer to him. When she was just a few feet away from him he met her. Jonathan held his arm out and Lucy placed her arm in his. They walked the rest of the way together.

The minister began speaking. When the minister asked the question who gives this woman, Ruth took it upon herself to give Lucy away. When they got to the ring exchange Lucy was surprised that Jonathan had them. She looked down as he put them on her. She thought they were absolutely breath taking. The two recited their wedding vows.

The minister then asked if there was anyone for any reason that they should not be married please speak now or forever hold your peace. Jonathan looked at his friend.

After a few seconds the minister pronounced them husband and wife. Ruth lifted Lucy's veil back. Jonathan looked at her. All Lucy's fears erased when she saw the look in his eyes. She knew he loved her. Jonathan bent down and kissed her. After a few seconds his friend tapped his shoulder and said save it for the honeymoon. Everyone laughed. The couple was congratulated...........

The group went up to their suite. Jonathan ordered room service. After ordering food Jonathan and Lucy excused themselves. As they were changing clothes Jonathan walked over to Lucy, put his arms around her waist and kissed her. For a few minutes they were lost. As Jonathan moved her towards the bed Lucy placed her hands between them and told him that they had guest. He smiled provocatively at her and then began kissing her again. Lucy protested and Jonathan stopped. He gave her a hurt look and then began dressing.

When they were finished dressing the couple returned to their guest. The group clapped when they reentered the room. The food had been delivered. The group mingled and ate. As it got late the group left, leaving the couple to themselves. Lucy exclaimed that they did not have any clothes. Nonchalantly Jonathan said they could purchase them on their honeymoon. The couple gathered what few things they had and left the hotel. They placed their things in the back seat of the car. The couple got into the car.

As Jonathan drove to the airport Lucy thought of the day. She tried to relive the events of her wedding. Lucy could not believe what had transpired in just a few hours. She leaned her head back, hoping this was not a dream......................

After they arrived at the airport Jonathan parked the car and they exited the vehicle. They walked quickly to the airport entrance. Lucy was surprised when they were able to walk pass the crowd.........

Once passed security they had forty-five minutes before boarding. Lucy saw a clothing store. She decided to look in it while Jonathan walked over to talk with the crew.

Shortly after the flight began to call for boarding Jonathan went to get Lucy. She was at the counter getting ready to purchase some items. Jonathan pulled out his debit card and told the cashier to take it out of it. Lucy tried to protest, but Jonathan insisted, saying that she was his wife now and he would take care of all her needs. The cashier looked at Lucy and smiled. She took the card and swiped it. The cashier placed the items in a bag and thanked them.

The couple left the store. Jonathan showed his identification and tickets to the airline personnel. The crew let him through. He told them that Lucy was his wife. They allowed her through as well. They sat three seats back in first class. Lucy was impressed. She had never flown before and to be in first class was a plus. Lucy looked out of the window.................

When the flight got on its way Lucy watched as the plane taxied the runway and then finally took off. Once the plane had gotten on its way the flight attendants began serving the first class passengers. Jonathan toasts his bride.

The day came over Lucy and she leaned her head back. Lucy fell asleep. Lucy slept throughout the flight.................

As the women drove back home Constance thought about the ceremony. She wondered if one day she and Paul would make that step. She wondered what he was doing.............

When Lucy awakened the plane was touching down. She was happy. Lucy tried hard not to let Jonathan know that she was not feeling well.

After exiting the airplane Lucy told Jonathan that she had to go to the rest room. He lightly kissed her. She smiled and then hurriedly walked to the rest room. Lucy tried not to touch anything. She leaned over and began throwing up. She was careful not to get any on herself. When she had nothing left in her stomach Lucy flushed the toilet and walked out of the stall. She took paper towels and washed her face. Lucy rinsed her mouth out. Still feeling queasy Lucy went into a store that was near the bathroom and purchased some crackers. She opened them and ate one. Lucy placed her hand on her stomach. She tried to get normal. When Jonathan saw her he became concerned. He asked if she was alright. Lucy told him that it was nothing to worry about. She told him that it was drinking on an empty stomach. As they walked through the airport Jonathan saw a restaurant. He guided her in it and asked what she wanted to eat. Lucy ordered a light breakfast.

When it came she sipped on the tea. Jonathan was on the phone most of the time that they sat in the restaurant. When Lucy had eaten all she was going to eat the couple left. Jonathan led her out of the airport to an awaiting car. They got in. Lucy leaned back onto Jonathan. He held her trying to comfort Lucy. She drifted off to sleep.........

Paul left Constance's house and headed back home. He thought of their lovemaking. Paul became aroused. He called Betsy. She met him at his home. She got out of the car when she saw him. They entered his home. As soon as she closed the door Paul and Betsy removed their clothes. She laid on the couch. He turned her over........................

When he was done he paid her and she left. Paul straightened up his house. He went into his bedroom and fell asleep..

A half hour later the driver parked. Jonathan paid the driver. He opened the door. Jonathan placed one arm under Lucy and pulled her to him. She awakened. He told her to go back to sleep. Lucy wrapped her arms around his neck. He lifted her out of the car. The driver grabbed the bag of clothes Lucy had purchased from the store in the airport. He handed the bag to Jonathan. Jonathan thanked the driver and then walked into the hotel. He checked in and then exited the building. Jonathan walked to a bungalow. Lucy told him that she could walk, but he insisted on carrying her.

When they made it to their bungalow Jonathan put his swipe card in the door and then opened it. He carried her through the rooms until he made it to the bedroom. Jonathan placed her gently onto the bed. He kissed her softly and told her to get some rest. Jonathan left the room. He closed the door behind himself. As Lucy lay in bed she looked around the room. She had never seen any room so beautiful. Lucy touched the covers. They were soft, like silk. The pillow she laid her head on was firm, yet so comfortable. The bed felt like nothing she had ever laid on. She soon drifted off to sleep...............

Lucy was only sleep for a half hour when she awakened. Lucy looked around and then realized where she was. She sat up thinking how this was her honeymoon and refused to sleep through it.

Lucy eased out of bed. She looked at herself in the full-length mirror. She tried to smooth her hair back, with no luck. Lucy thought how she must look a sight to her husband. Lucy smiled thinking of that word, husband. It sounded better than any word she could think of. Lucy went into the connecting bathroom. She returned to the bedroom to look for her bag, but it was not there. She thought of venturing out to look for it, but did not want Jonathan to see her like she was. Lucy returned to the bathroom, removed her clothes and got into the shower. She let the warm water run down her body. It felt soothing to her. She put her face in the water and then her head. Lucy turned around and backed into the shower. For a few minutes she stood under the warm water running down her body. She then began to wash her body. Lucy used the shampoo that was in the bathroom. When she had finished washing every inch of her body Lucy rinsed off and then turned the shower off. She dried off and then proceeded to style her hair with the blow drier she found in the bathroom. Lucy wrapped a towel around herself. She looked into the bathroom's mirror and found herself to be presentable. Lucy walked through another door leading into the living area. She smiled when she saw Jonathan sitting upright in a chair asleep. Lucy slowly walked over to him. When she was close Lucy sat on his lap. She smoothed her hand along the side of his face and then leaned in to kiss him. He wrapped his arms around her and returned her kiss. As the kiss became intense he stopped.

"I thought you weren't feeling well."

"This is our honeymoon, I can be sick later."

Jonathan looked into his new brides eyes. He did not see sickness. He saw desire. Desire he hoped would always be there. He kissed her again. Jonathan put his arms firmly around her body and picked her up. He carried her into the bedroom. Still kissing her Jonathan slowly and gently laid his bride onto the bed. He stopped kissing Lucy and looked down at her. Jonathan smoothed his hand down her body. Lucy shivered. Jonathan asked if she was cold. Lucy shook her head no. She held her arms out. Jonathan went into them…………..

Hours later Jonathan asked Lucy if she wanted to go out to eat. She jumped out of bed. She went into the living room and got her bag. Lucy pulled out a dress and pair of shoes. Jonathan sat up and said, "I guess you do." Lucy placed the clothes on the chair and walked over to Jonathan. She held her hand out to him. Jonathan took it. Lucy led him into the bathroom. While continuing to hold Jonathan's hand she used her free one to turn on the shower. She felt the water. Lucy stepped into the shower, bringing Jonathan in with her. She picked up the soap and rubbed it in her hand building up lather. Jonathan looked on. Jonathan was turned on by this new woman. When she had built up enough lather Lucy began smoothing it over her husband's body. Lucy smiled as she looked into his eyes. She had never done this before. Caught in Jonathan's desire Lucy let him take over.............

Chapter 5

Sometime later the couple turned the shower off and got out. They dried each other off. While Lucy styled her hair Jonathan laid back down..................................

When she was done Lucy returned to the bedroom where Jonathan had fallen asleep. She walked over to him and kissed him. He grabbed her and kissed her passionately. Lucy returned the passion and then stopped abruptly. She told him to get up and dress. He continued to hold her. She told him if they did not get up they would not make it to the restaurant. When this did not faze him Lucy told him that she was hungry. Jonathan kissed her again and then released her. Lucy got up and picked her dress up. She ran the iron over it quickly.

Lucy pulled it up onto her body and smoothed it. She noticed Jonathan watching her. Lucy liked the attention and hoped that he would always look at her this way. Jonathan asked if she was ready. Lucy gave herself a quick look over and then walked over to him. Jonathan picked up the key card and put his arm around her. They walked out of the door. The couple proceeded to walk down the beach. The restaurant was not too far down from their Villa. Jonathan held Lucy close. Lucy liked the way it felt being held by Jonathan. She felt secure.

When they arrived at the restaurant the hostess escorted them to a table with a beautiful view. After the hostess left them the waiter approached them. He asked what they would be drinking. Lucy asked for juice. Jonathan looked at her, but did not comment. He ordered soda. After the waiter had walked away Jonathan asked Lucy was she feeling alright. Lucy told him that she was feeling wonderful. She explained about them not using any protection and if by chance she was or to get pregnant she did not want the baby to have any problems. After telling him this a concerned look came over her face. Jonathan asked what was wrong. Lucy told him that she was sorry that they had not discussed children. Jonathan took her hand and brought it to his mouth. He kissed it and then confided that he had thought about it. When their drinks returned Jonathan held his soda up and made a toast to new beginnings. Lucy gladly drank to it. They ordered their food.

Lucy was famished by the time the food was brought to them. She ate the entire meal and ordered dessert. A band played in the back of the restaurant. After dinner the couple went back there. Jonathan put his hand out and asked if he could have this dance. She took his hand. Jonathan spun Lucy around and then brought her close to him. He held her tight. Lucy rested her head on his shoulder. They swayed to the music. The couple was lost in their own world where only they existed. They danced until the leader of the band announced that the club was closed. He had to say it twice before they heard him. The couple asked for their forgiveness and left. Jonathan and Lucy returned to their Villa..................

The next day the couple got up early, had breakfast and toured the island.

That night they returned to the club. Jonathan and Lucy danced all night. After the club closed the two walked along the beach. Lucy could not help feeling like she was dreaming………………………..

The next morning Jonathan and Lucy went down to the beach and stayed there the entire day……………………………

When it got late the couple returned to the club. The workers knew them by name and treated them like family. Jonathan told them that it was their last night. The couple danced until the restaurant closed. The band played one last song and dedicated it to Jonathan and Lucy.

After leaving the restaurant the couple walked along the beach. Jonathan let go of Lucy's hand and then placed his arm around her. He pulled her close. Lucy looked out into the ocean and wondered how their lives will be when they return home……….

Jonathan interrupted her thoughts.

"I know what you're thinking."

"What am I thinking?"

"You're wondering if we'll feel the same when we get home."

"Where will we live?"

"We can stay in my condo for a little while and then look for a house."

"Jonathan I'm afraid."

"Of what?"

"This is so perfect."

"You don't believe in perfection?"

"I've never seen it." Lucy placed both arms around his waist and laid her head on his chest. "Don't ever stop loving me."

Jonathan held Lucy tighter. Jonathan brought her face to look up to his. He looked down at Lucy.

"Sweetheart I will always love you and I will never do anything to hurt you. Trust me Lovely Lucy." She looked at him curious. "What?"

"You called me Lovely Lucy."

"You don't like it?"

"No, I like it." She smiled. It sounds nice. I mean your voice. It sounds nice hearing you say it."

"Oh you like my voice." Jonathan kissed her. The kiss became fiery. He lowered her to the ground.

"What are you doing?"

Jonathan did not speak. He continued kissing her. Lucy looked around to see if anyone was around. The beach was empty. She placed her hand behind his head. Jonathan was lost. Lucy knew there was no coming back. She allowed herself to let go.....................

Lucy lay under Jonathan holding onto him. Water rushed up to them. Jonathan tried to shield her. They got up and fixed their clothes. Jonathan and Lucy walked arm in arm the rest of the way to their Villa. The couple walked in and closed the door behind themselves.................

Chapter 6

The next day the couple heard a knock on the door. The couple looked at the clock and then jumped up. Jonathan ran to the door. He told the driver that they would be right out. The couple quickly dressed. Lucy gathered what few things she brought and they were on their way...................

As they traveled to the airport Lucy watched the beauty of the city quickly disappear behind her.........................

When they arrived at the airport Jonathan grabbed Lucy's bags and they went inside. The couple hurried through the airport checkpoints to the gate. The plane had begun boarding. Jonathan and Lucy were able to board. Lucy did not sleep this time. She and Jonathan talked about their future....................

By the time they had arrived back in Philly the couple had mapped out their life together. When the plane landed the couple prepared themselves to exit.

Once the doors opened the couple exited the plane and headed to the parking deck. They got into Jonathan's car and he drove off. Lucy laid her head on his shoulder. She was excited about being married. She told Jonathan as much. He returned the sentiment. When they arrived at his condominium he parked the car. They exited the car. Jonathan lifted Lucy into his arms and carried her into the apartment. Jonathan placed their things in his bedroom..........................

As time passed the couple adjusted to their new life. They often talked about purchasing a house, but decided to wait until the baby was born.

Jonathan and Lucy went on walks around the complex if he got off work early. Lucy enjoyed these walks. They often held hands or Jonathan placed his arm around her shoulders or waist. He was so loving. She felt secure. Most nights Jonathan was home and Lucy had dinner warm and waiting for him. Although Jonathan told Lucy that she could stay home, she decided to work six months before resigning.

When she was six months pregnant Lucy handed in her resignation. They threw her a farewell party. Lucy thought she would miss work, but during the day Jonathan called her whenever he got a chance, with sometimes his co-workers and friends making jokes about him being sprung.

At night after making love he held her providing the warmth of his body and security of his love. Before falling asleep every night Lucy often wondered if this happiness could last.....................................

Lucy prepared dinner. She set the table. Lucy was now six months pregnant. She was not showing, but could feel the baby moving.

She was getting hungry, but wanted to wait for Jonathan to come home.....................

It was getting late so Lucy decided to eat. She frequently looked at the time.......... Several hours later there still was not any word from Jonathan. She called his cell phone, but he did not answer it. Lucy became worried. Jonathan had always called if he was going to be late. She decided to call the airline that he worked for.

When the person answered the phone Lucy explained who she was and asked if Jonathan's flight had come in. Lucy noticed the hesitation when she asked about the flight that Jonathan was flying. Then the woman told her that there had been trouble. Lucy's heart dropped. Lucy questioned the woman, but was not able to get much from her. Lucy hung up the phone. She cleared the dishes from the dining room table. As she cleaned the kitchen Lucy prayed. She felt sick. Tears rolled down her face. Lucy called her friend Ruth. They talked for a few minutes and then Ruth offered to come over. Lucy told her that she did not have to, but Ruth insisted.............................

Ruth came over. She tried to convince Lucy that Jonathan would be alright. Ruth told Lucy that she was going to stay the night. Lucy welcomed her presence. Lucy and Ruth sat in the living room. Lucy held the phone................

After several hours the phone rang. Lucy jumped. She answered the phone. As she listened tears filled her eyes and rolled down her face. Ruth sat frozen wondering what was being said. She noticed Lucy holding her stomach. Ruth could no longer watch. She asked Lucy if she was okay. She then walked over to her and took the phone. Ruth explained to the person that she was a close friend. The gentleman confided that Jonathan's plane ran into a storm and they are unable to detect it. Ruth placed her hand over her mouth afraid to make a sound and upset Lucy. When she got off of the phone Ruth placed her arm around Lucy. Ruth knew nothing to say. Tears ran down her face as she tried to comfort her friend.....................

As days and weeks and then a month went by Ruth stayed close to her friend. Ruth convinced Lucy to sign up for Lamaze and promised to be her coach. It was discovered at Lucy's seventh month visit that she was carrying twins. Ruth tried to keep Lucy's spirits up........................

Lucy tried to concentrate on keeping herself and her babies healthy. She talked to them often telling them about their father. During this time she sometimes thought of how she really didn't know very much about him, but one thing she knew was that she loved him so much.............................

She once found a small photo album and wondered who the people were in the photos.

Lucy converted the guest room into a nursery. She often thought of getting a house, but was afraid to move because Jonathan would not know where they were when he returned...........................

In Lucy's last month she decided to copy the pictures in Jonathan's photo album. She made two mobiles out of them and placed them over the babies' cribs...............

Several weeks later Lucy woke up feeling pressure. She placed her bag in the car. She cleaned her house and then went over the babies' rooms.....................

By afternoon she decided to lay down. She felt sharp pains in her back. Lucy placed a pillow under her legs to alleviate the pain. She finally drifted off to sleep. Lucy dreamed of Jonathan:

"They were walking along the beach. He held her hand tight. Lucy asked him where he had been. He only answered I love you. Lucy looked over and he was gone. She called out to him. A sharp pain came over her and she grabbed her stomach. The ocean turned red. She looked on wondering what was going on."

Lucy awakened and realized her water had broken. She called Ruth. Lucy tried to keep busy while she waited for Ruth to arrive...................................

When Ruth arrived the person at the gate opened it and she drove in. The person at the gate alerted Lucy of Ruth's arrival. Lucy left out of the condominium. She walked slowly down the hall. Just as Ruth approached the front of the building Lucy was opening the door. Ruth put her hand out to help her. She started for her car, but Lucy told her she wanted to go in her own. Ruth obliged her. They got into the car. Ruth pulled off. Ruth coached Lucy on her breathing................

When they finally arrived at the hospital Ruth helped Lucy in and once she was settled Ruth went to move the car..............................

When she returned to Lucy's side they were getting ready to take her to the birthing room.

Lucy was instructed to push. After a few pushes the first baby was born. To Lucy's delight it was a boy. Lucy began pushing again. Again after several pushes a second baby was born. This one would be a girl. Tears streamed down Lucy's eyes. Ruth placed her arm around her friend. Through a muffled sound Ruth understood Lucy to say, "He would be so proud."

Ruth said she knew. Lucy was taken to her room. A little while later the babies were brought into Lucy's room. Ruth brought them closer to her. Lucy sat up and eased herself out of bed. She looked over at her babies. Lucy eyes filled up with tears. Ruth looking over at Lucy felt bad for her friend. She walked over to her friend and placed her arm around Lucy's shoulders. Lucy bent down and picked her son up. She kissed him and held him close. Lucy whispered in his ear that his father loved him. She then laid him back down and did the same to her baby girl. Lucy walked back to her bed and laid down. Ruth told her she was going to leave.

She wanted to give the new family time to get acquainted.

After she left Lucy watched her babies sleeping until she fell asleep. While she slept Lucy dreamed of Jonathan:

"Jonathan had come home. She hugged him. Lucy asked where he had been. He did not answer. He looked over and saw the babies. Jonathan smiled. Lucy knew that he thought the babies were beautiful. **Lucy heard crying**."

She awakened. JJ, what she decided to call her son was awake and crying. Lucy picked him up. He was hungry. She went back to the bed and leaned back. She opened her shirt and began feeding him. As he ate Lucy smiled thinking how he was going to eat like his father. She leaned her head back and thought how lonely she felt..............

When JJ had finished eating Lucy rubbed his back. She changed his diaper, kissed him and then laid him back in his bassinet. Just as she laid JJ down Joanna awakened. Lucy picked her up and laid back in the bed. She began feeding Joanna. Lucy closed her eyes. She thought of her babies. Lucy began to pray, thanking God for blessing her with these beautiful babies. She drifted off to sleep. Lucy slept soundly for several hours……….. When she awakened Lucy realized that she had fallen asleep holding Joanna. She smiled down at her baby girl. Lucy smoothed her hand over the baby's head……….…….

The nurse came into the room. She smiled and took Lucy's vitals. She complimented Lucy on her babies and then left.

An hour later the doctor came in. He read Lucy's chart and checked her vitals. He asked Lucy how she was doing and then told her that she was being released. Lucy was happy about this.

After the doctor left Lucy called Ruth. Ruth was at work and told Lucy she would be there after work, explaining that she did not have any time left. Lucy told her not to worry about it and said that she was just grateful for her assistance.

When the women hung up the phone JJ had awakened again. Lucy nursed him and again changed his diaper. She held him a while longer and then dressed him in the clothes that she had purchased for him to wear home. She laid him down and then picked up Joanna. She dressed her as well, laid the baby back down and then dressed herself.

With the babies sleeping soundly and she being pack up and ready to go Lucy sat in a chair by the window in her room. She stared out of it. Lucy looked on as couples left with their babies. Lucy looked back at her babies wishing Jonathan were there. She talked out laud as if he was there telling him to come back to her and their babies. After some time Lucy heard a knock on the door. She told them to come in. The nurse came in. She gave Lucy some papers to sign. After Lucy signed the papers the nurse gave her a copy of them and then left.

A few minutes later Ruth came into the room. She hugged her friend. A nurse came in behind her. She was pushing a wheel chair. At first Lucy protested, but the nurse insisted explaining that it was hospital policy. Lucy sat in the chair. The two women placed the babies in Lucy's arms. She held the babies close to her. Ruth pushed her friend outside of the hospital as the nurse walked by their side.

Once outside, Ruth left Lucy for a few minutes to get the car. She returned shortly and pulled in front of Lucy. She got out of the car and walked over to Lucy. She took JJ and put him in his car seat. She then returned to Lucy and then took Joanna. Ruth placed the baby in her car seat and secured her. Ruth drove the new family home.

Once they had settled in Lucy thanked Ruth and than told her that she didn't have to stay. Lucy added that she and the babies would be fine.

At first Ruth protested, but Lucy explained her reasons and after some time she prevailed. Ruth hugged Lucy. Lucy assured Ruth that she and the babies would be fine. Ruth was hesitant, but she honored Lucy's decision. Lucy walked her to the door and watched as she got into her car.

After Ruth drove away Lucy went back into the building. She secured the door and went to the nursery. She sat down in the rocking chair. She looked on as her babies slept. Lucy fell asleep in the chair. She slept there until she heard crying. Lucy looked up and saw JJ moving. She got up and picked him up. Lucy kissed him on the forehead and then sat down. She began to nurse him. Lucy smoothed her hand over his head as he nursed. When he had finished eating she changed his diaper, but did not put him down. Lucy rocked him until he fell asleep. She held him close to her until Joanna awakened. Lucy placed JJ down and then picked Joanna up. She nursed her and then changed her diaper. Lucy brushed her hair and put a bow in it. She put Joanna down and then left the nursery. She went into her bedroom. Lucy looked around and felt lonely.....................

Lucy began spending much of her time in the nursery, many times sleeping in the rocking chair.

After several months Lucy contacted a realtor. Lucy could not deal with staying in Jonathan's condo any longer. It was filled with his presence, which made her unhappy. She thought by moving to a new home she would be able to move on.................

Several months went by before Lucy was able to find what she thought was the perfect home for her and the babies.

Lucy closed on the babies' birthday.

After the closing Ruth met her at the condo. Lucy had purchased a cake. She had invited Raymond and her other friends. They sang happy birthday to the twins. The group had become like aunts and Raymond an uncle to the twins. Raymond came over often to offer his assistance. He knew his friend would have wanted him to look after his family. Lucy was grateful for this. She welcomed a male's presence and help with the babies.

After the party was over Raymond stayed behind. It was still early in the evening. Raymond offered to help her straighten up. She declined his assistance, telling him that she appreciated his company. She offered him a drink. While she straightened up and finished packing the two talked, mostly about Jonathan. Raymond had a few more drinks. When she decided to rest Lucy sat next to Raymond. He saw the sadness in her eyes. Raymond put his arm around her. Lucy laid her head on his shoulder and closed her eyes. She thought how good it felt to be held. Raymond caressed her hair, wanting to comfort his friend's wife. He had become to know her and understood why his friend had fallen for her. They stayed quiet for a little while. Raymond realized he had too much to drink. He asked if he could sleep on the couch and promised not to be a bother. Lucy told him that he was more than welcomed to stay. She offered him a bed to sleep in, but he told her that he would be fine. She got up and lightly kissed him good night.

Lucy went upstairs. She checked on the twins and then went to her room. She laid down and fell asleep with her clothes still on. She began to dream:

"Lucy was in her new home. There was a knock on the door. The door opened and standing there was Jonathan. He was wearing his job uniform. Lucy reached out to him, but he was too far away. She called out to him. He did not answer, or move. Lucy felt herself move towards him, but he seemed to move away. She called out. Tears drenched her face."

She heard someone call her name and awakened.

When she awakened Raymond was holding her. He asked if she was alright. She told him about her dream. Lucy began to cry. Raymond held her in his arms. He felt bad for her. Raymond held her until she fell asleep. He laid her down gently and then left the room. Raymond walked down the hall and checked on the babies. When he entered the nursery JJ was moving around. He rubbed the baby's back. When the baby settled down Raymond left the room. When he returned to the couch he thought of Lucy. He thought how awful it was for such a beautiful woman to be left alone and how difficult it must be for her being young without a man. He thought of his friend. Raymond wondered if his friend was dead or injured and could not get back to his family................

As the sun began coming up Raymond fell back to sleep...........................

Raymond awakened when he heard the men talking as they walked in the front door. Raymond stood up. He apologized to Lucy for over sleeping. She told him that he had nothing to be sorry for. Raymond addressed the movers and took over. He helped Lucy place the twins in her car. He tapped the car after closing the door. Lucy drove off. She looked in her rear view mirror, thinking that it would be the last time that she will see the condo............

As Lucy drove to her new home she thought about her life and all she had been through. She thought of the men that she had come in contact with, the few boyfriends and then of Paul. For a second she wondered what he was doing and then she frowned. She thought of the night that she left him. Lucy remembered the manager at the hotel she ended up staying in. She smiled thinking of the care he provided. Lucy also thought of their time together. She wondered if he did that often.

As she continued to drive JJ whimpered. She looked back and smiled saying out loud, "Oh you're looking out for daddy? No worries son, I'm waiting for your daddy to return." As if he knew what she was talking about JJ smiled. Lucy thought of Jonathan. She thought of the night they first met. She remembered how she thought he was too young for her. Lucy felt lonely...............

Jonathan had been gone for almost two years now. She had not considered that he would not have shown up. Lucy wondered if he had in fact been killed. Her eyes became glassy. She thought of how he made her feel and became aroused. Lucy feared she would never feel that again. Lucy remembered how happy Jonathan was when she agreed to marry him and excited when she told him that she was pregnant.

Lucy pulled up in front of her new home. She had a good feeling. Lucy turned the car off and got out. She walked to the side of the car and opened the door. Lucy took Joanna out and then walked to the other side. She opened the door and took JJ out. She carried the two on either side. Lucy managed to put the key in the door and open it. She knew the cleaning company had been there.

Lucy carried the children on her hips while walking through the house. She went upstairs and peered into each room. Lucy went back downstairs. The doorbell rang. She went to answer it. It was the moving crew. She opened the door wider. The movers began bringing the furniture in from the condo.

Lucy had purchased new furniture for some of the rooms. She donated some of Jonathan's furniture to the veterans. She kept his bedroom set and put it in the guest room. She kept his clothes hoping he would someday return to her. Lucy showed the movers where everything was to go. Raymond helped put the babies' beds together and Lucy put the babies down. She closed their doors and went downstairs.

Lucy went into the living room where Raymond was talking to one of the movers. She gave instructions as to where to put everything. She combined some new pieces with some of Jonathan's furniture. Raymond observed Lucy, finally realizing that she was in love with his friend. He had not believed it in the beginning, thinking she was possibly a gold digger. He knew his friend was very kind and had been taken advantage of before. Raymond was beginning to feel an obligation to stand by this woman.......................

Chapter 7

Raymond became a surrogate uncle. He came around as much as he could to make sure Lucy and the children were doing alright. On Occasion he came over and had Sunday dinner with them.....

Two years went by. Raymond began dating. He brought the woman by to meet Lucy. Lucy was uncomfortable because when Raymond introduced them the woman's response was "So you're the one who takes up my man's time."

It was obvious that the woman was jealous of Lucy. Lucy felt inclined to apologize to the statement. The woman didn't say anything, instead she sat closer to Raymond and wrapped her arm around his. Lucy observed the woman and thought her very pretty, but did not think she good enough for Raymond..

Through the night the women made polite conversation and both knew it was strained. Surprisingly to Lucy, Raymond had not noticed.

When he and his lady friend got up to leave Raymond hugged Lucy and kissed her lightly on the lips. The woman looked on and Lucy could feel her contempt. Lucy graciously said it was nice to meet the woman and then the woman and Raymond left.........................

Several months went by. Lucy had not heard from Raymond. She figured it was on account of his girlfriend.....................……..

The children were quickly growing. Lucy decided to send them to daycare. The children enjoyed their time in school.

Although she was pleased at their progression this gave Lucy time on her hand that she did not know what to do with.

As the days flew by Lucy began wondering what she should do with this time..............

"Good morning."

In a hoarse voice, "Good morning nurse."

"How is my patient?"

"About the same."

"How are your legs?"

"I try to stand on them every day."

"Maybe you should listen to the doctor."

"Then I am defeated."

"We have wheel chairs."

"You're referring to those wooden things you give to patients who have given up?"

"We are a poor people here. We do our best."

"I know and I am thankful for your care. It's just so frustrating not knowing who I am."

"I understand. I wish we had someone to call for you. You sure you don't remember where you're from?"

"I'm only sure of a name in my head.

"The authorities weren't able to find anything in the wreckage. The plane broke in many pieces. There was wreckage all over."

"Was there any other survivors?"

"What I gathered you washed on the shore. You were knocked from the plane. You are the only one that ended up here. The others were on the mainland."

"You've over exhausted yourself. Get some rest."

He laid his head back...

Lucy decided to do some of the things that she had always wanted to do but was never able. After dropping the children off at school Lucy went on the computer and downloaded information on museums..............................

After she had retrieved information on the museums and sorted the ones that interest her Lucy began visiting them. Raymond had broken up with his girlfriend by then, so he sometimes accompanied her. She enjoyed these moments. While Lucy enjoyed her trips, sometimes she became lonely. She reached out to her friends occasionally, but hated to monopolize their time. She was surprised when Ruth told her that Constance did not go out with them any longer. Ruth informed her that Constance had a man and he took up most of her time. Lucy was surprised and expressed her delight in Constance finding someone special.

The other women were still into the club scene. Ruth often invited both Constance and Lucy, but they declined. Lucy was no longer interested in going out to clubs because they reminded her of Jonathan. Lucy did not want to dance or enjoy music. She had lost that part of herself, since Jonathan was no longer there…………………………………...

"Good morning Mr. Mills."

"Good morning doctor."

"Today you are free."

"I don't feel so free. I'm still not walking the way I would like to."

"You've worked so hard. You now know your name. You have made me believe that you will walk with very little restriction one day."

"What I need to do is get my memory back and return to where ever I'm from."

"What about this Lovely Lucy?"

"That's all I have. I believe she is someone special or was in my life. Do you think she'll be still waiting for me?"

"I know it's been five years, but you must concentrate on getting your health better."

"Thank you doctor. I will."

The nurse named Sally came into the room. She asked Jonathan if he was ready. He stood on one crutch and walked out with Sally. She helped him into her car and then got in. She drove through the mountains....................

When they arrived at her home something flashed in his mind, but he was unable to make since of it.................................

As the days, weeks and then months passed Jonathan began walking better. He began remembering bits and pieces of his past, but still did not remember where these memories originated.

A year passed. Sally expressed her feelings for him. Jonathan was hesitant, confiding that he believed there was someone possibly waiting for him. He confessed that he could not promise that he could ever feel for her what she felt for him. Sally told him that she would accept that, but secretly hoped that one day he would feel for her what she felt for him. Sally did not rush him to share her bedroom. She had an extra room and this is where Jonathan slept.

They went on walks to strengthen his legs. Although she worked with him on strengthening his mind, Sally secretly hoped that he would not regain his memory.........

New Year's Eve Sally and Jonathan shared an intimate dinner together. She hoped that this would begin their new life together. They sat out on her porch and watched the ocean. She brought out drinks for them to toast the New Year. When they heard and saw the fireworks Sally held her glass up and said, "To us." She clicked her glass to his. She sipped hers and told Jonathan to drink his. He slowly brought the drink to his lips. He looked out into the ocean, wondering who Lovely Lucy was. He thought of this woman many times as he looked out into the ocean. He often dreamed of her, never being able to see her face.

Sally kissed Jonathan on the lips, breaking his concentration. He looked at her.

"Happy New Year."

"I'm sorry happy New Year. I am tired. Do you mind if I turn in?"

"No."

Sally had lied. She had hoped that they would begin the New Year with Jonathan deciding to move on with his life. She wondered how long could he go without sex. She really wanted to be with this man. She found him very handsome and had a great body. She thought him very intelligent. She had not dated for some time, spending much of her time with Jonathan at the hospital. She soon fell for him. She felt that he was a good man. Sally wished that he could feel for her what he obviously felt for this mystery woman. Sally got up. She walked with him to his room. Sally said good night. She then went to her room. Sally undressed and then laid down. She laid in bed thinking of Jonathan. It was some time before she was able to fall asleep.

Jonathan layed in bed thinking about Sally's expression of her feelings. He knew she was attracted to him when she asked him to come home with her. Jonathan went because he had nowhere else to go. He felt bad knowing that she obviously felt something for him, but he was afraid of allowing himself to begin a relationship. He believed that one day he might regain his memory and someone would get hurt............................

Time passed slowly for Jonathan. He struggled everyday watching how Sally looked at him and knowing he hurt her every time he denied her...........................

It was ten years since Jonathan had disappeared. The twins were turning ten. Lucy threw a party for them. Lucy watched how her children were growing quickly. She could not believe how time had flown by, yet seemed slow as well. She looked at her son. He looked so much like his father. Ruth interrupted her thoughts. She told her that it was getting late. Lucy apologized for the delay and went into the dining room. She lit the candles. Everyone stood around the table and sang happy birthday to the twins. Lucy had separate cakes for the twins and they each had their own set of friends.

When the group finished singing the twins looked at each other, smiled and then blew out their candles. Everyone clapped. The cakes were cut and handed out to the guest.

Shortly after everyone finished eating their cake the children opened their gifts.

After the last gift was opened Lucy thanked everyone for coming. The guest began leaving. Constance offered to stay behind to help her straighten up. Lucy told her that she didn't have to, but Constance insisted......................................

A half hour after the last guest left the doorbell rang. Constance said that she would get it and stated that she was expecting someone. Constance went to the door. She opened it. Constance hugged the man at the door. Constance asked him in. The man came in. The twins had gone up to their rooms. Lucy went to see who was at the door. She stopped abruptly. Lucy could not believe standing in her foyer arm in arm was Constance and Paul. Lucy looked unbelieving. Paul with his beautiful smile said good afternoon. Lucy did not want Constance to know that she had been in a relationship with this man. She nodded her head. Constance introduced them. She hugged Lucy and told her that it was time for her to leave. Lucy for that brief moment thought of telling Constance her dealings with Paul, but then thought better of it. She thought that maybe he had changed. Lucy thanked Constance for coming and then told her to be safe.

Once she was alone Lucy continued cleaning her house. She began thinking how much she missed Jonathan. She locked up her house and went up to her bedroom. Lucy checked on her children. They were asleep. Lucy went to bed. She laid in bed thinking about Constance and Paul. Although it took a while Lucy finally drifted off to sleep...

Constance and Paul got into his car. Paul pulled off. He drove several blocks away and then pulled over.

"What are you doing? I thought you were going to ask her."

"Paul why can't I be enough? I do everything you ask of me. We have to stop this. Paul you need help."

"Exactly. I need you to help me get what I need."

"Paul are you still in love with her?"

"I told you that you are special to me and I need you. Isn't that enough?"

"I love you Paul. I don't like you having sex with all these women."

"You're not enough. You have to recover all the time. I need sex when I need it and right now I need to do this. I need to be with Lucy."

"Paul please don't make me do this."

"You said that you would. You said that you loved me."

"I do."

"I don't think so. All you think about is yourself."

"Ok Paul I will do this."

Paul turned the car around and drove back to Lucy's home. Paul got out first and then with hesitance Constance got out of the car. She and Paul walked up to Lucy's door.

As she looked at Paul Constance rang the doorbell.

The ringing of the doorbell awakened Lucy. She looked at the clock next to her bedside. It was three in the morning. She put on her housecoat and went downstairs. Lucy turned on the hall light. She opened the door. Standing there was Constance and Paul. Lucy asked what was going on. Constance asked if they could come in. Lucy stepped back. The couple entered her house. Constance asked if they could sit and talk. Lucy not wanting to seem rude led them into the living room. She told them to sit. Constance asked for a drink. Lucy looked at her curiously. She told Constance that there was no liquor in her house. Lucy announced that it was late and told Constance to get on with what she had come there for. Constance looked at Paul and then cleared her throat. She began by asking Lucy had she found anyone since Jonathan. Again Lucy looked at Constance curious without acknowledging Paul's presence.

"Why are you here this time of night asking me a question like this?"

"Lucy you don't have to pretend. I know you and Paul use to date. That is why we are here. We wanted someone we know."

"What are you talking about?"

"Since you don't have anyone and haven't been with anyone, we figured you may be missing a man's touch."

"Constance this is hardly the time to discuss this. Besides when I'm ready to date I will find my own...."

"You misunderstand."

"I guess I am."

"The kids are asleep right?"

"Yes. Why?"

"Paul wants to be with you."

Lucy stood up. Paul walked over to Lucy and smoothed the back of his hand down the side of her face. Lucy moved back.

"I think it's time for you to leave."

"I told you she won't want to do it."

"Lucy I know we parted on bad terms. I apologize for that." He moved closer to her. "Lucy I miss you. (Constance looked at him.) I am not asking you to come back to me, but I have been having this dream and I remember how good you were. Constance told me that your husband died, so you're all alone now."

"He's not dead. He's missing."

"I'm sorry." He looked at Constance. "I've been misinformed. All the better. I can keep you active until he returns."

"Aren't you with Constance?"

"She's alright with what I'm proposing."

"It's been over. There's nothing here for you Paul."

Constance walked behind Lucy. She put her hands on her shoulders.

"Lucy I'm with it. I want to please my man."

"Do you know what he's asking?"

"I do whatever it takes to please my man."

Lucy shrugged her shoulders and moved away from Constance.

"Get out of my house."

Paul walked up to her and picked Lucy up.

"Where is it?"

Constance quickly led Paul to the basement. He carried Lucy down the stairs. Lucy kicked and tried to wiggle her way out of his arms, but he was too strong. She did not call out, because she did not want her children to see what was going on. Once they were in the basement Paul held Lucy tighter.

"Tie her hands."

"Don't do it. Do not do this. Please."

Constance tied Lucy's hands behind her. She then went back upstairs, leaving Lucy alone with Paul.

Lucy yelled, "Constance don't let him do this."

Paul tried to kiss Lucy. She moved her head and tightened her mouth, keeping it closed. He kissed her lips gently telling her to relax. He told her that he was there to make her feel good. Lucy pleaded with him to no avail. Tears rolled down her face as Paul caressed her body. Paul caressed her body until it trembled with pleasure. He smiled as her body overrode her mind. He continued his pursuit and when he thought her ready joined her. She laid there, not moving, with eyes drenched from crying. Paul licked her tears telling her not to cry and asked doesn't it feel good.

"If I didn't know you I would think you were a virgin. You feel better than you did when we were together. Come on move with me, you'll feel even better."

Lucy stayed still. Again Paul felt her body react to his touch. He whispered in her ear how she could feel this way all the time if she wanted.

When Paul couldn't hold back any longer he stopped talking. Her body went with him. Paul collapsed remaining on top of her.

Once Paul gained his composure he looked at Lucy.

"Don't look like that. Didn't it feel good? Don't be like that."

Paul got up. He used the bathroom and then brought a towel and washed Lucy off.

With tears still streaming down her face she said, "Get off of me and untie me!"

Paul did as she asked. "Get out of my house! Paul don't ever come back here!"

Paul went up the stairs with Lucy following close behind.

When they arrived at the top of the stairs Constance was waiting. The look on Lucy's face made her apologize and quickly walk to the front door.

Paul arrogant as always told Lucy that if she ever needed anything she knew where she could reach him. She said, "Just go." Paul and Constance left.

Lucy got cleaning solution and returned to the basement. She sprayed her leather couch and began scrubbing it. She then sprayed Lysol on it. Lucy went into the bathroom down there and cleaned it and then poured bleach everywhere she thought Paul might have touched. She scanned her house spraying Lysol disinfectant all over everything. Lucy put the chemicals up and then went in to check on the children. They were still asleep and seemed to sleep through the night. She thanked God for that.

Lucy went into her bathroom. She turned the shower on. Lucy got in. She scrubbed her body for an hour. If not for the water coming from the shower her tears would have drenched her face. When Lucy thought that she had washed the night off Lucy turned the water off and stepped out of the shower. Lucy dried off and then went into her bedroom. Lucy put on a pair of jeans and a blouse. She then went down to fix breakfast...............

When it was done Lucy went up to wake the children. They got dressed and came down to the kitchen. Lucy watched the children eat. Joanna questioned her about her not eating. Lucy told her daughter she wasn't hungry................

When the children were finished eating they went back up to their room. Lucy called her doctor. She got the answering service. Lucy left a message that it was urgent for him to return her call...........................

Several hours later the doctor returned her call. Lucy explained briefly that she had unprotected sex and needed the morning after pill. When he was hesitant Lucy confided that it wasn't consensual. The doctor told Lucy that he would call the pharmacy. After getting off of the phone with the doctor Lucy told the children that they were to get ready ....

The children finished dressing and the family left..................

A half hour later Lucy pulled into the drug store parking lot. She and the children exited the car. They walked across the parking lot, the children chattering carefree, unknowing what their mother was going through. Lucy was happy that they had not awakened the night before and come looking for her.

They entered the store. The children ran over to the toy isle. Lucy went to the pharmacy. She gave her name. The prescription was ready. Lucy paid the co-pay and then went to find her children. The family left the store.............

Although Lucy was feeling tired, depressed and angry she didn't want the children to have to suffer. She decided to take them to the movies. When she told the children of her plans they were ecstatic. There was a movie that the children had talked about seeing. The children excitedly talked about the movie. Lucy smiled thinking how innocent they were. Her eyes became glossy. She fought back the tears. When she finally pulled into the parking lot of the movie theater Lucy had gotten herself together.

After parking the family exited the car and walked towards the theater. She paid for the tickets and they went in. The kids asked for snacks. When they had made it to the counter the kids ordered their snacks. Lucy purchased a water for herself. The family walked to the movie location. They sat down. While the children watched and laughed throughout the movie Lucy thought about her night. Tears formed in her eyes. She didn't know whether she was angry about the sexual assault, Constance bringing Paul there, knowing what he was going to do or her body's reaction. She excused herself and rushed out of the theater. Lucy went to her car and got in. She began to cry......................

Forty-five minutes went by. Someone knocked on her window. Lucy looked through tear-filled eyes at the gentleman. The man asked if she was okay. At first Lucy just stared at the man. He gave her a few minutes and then repeated his question. Lucy couldn't keep it in. Through tears and distorted words the man was able to make out what she said. The information was more than he expected. He placed his hand down on the window. He calmly told her that she should get herself checked out. Lucy explained again particulars of the event. The man explained what he meant. The man noticed a light went on in her head and then fear formed over her face. The man told her where a health center was. She thanked him. He gave her his card and introduced himself as Lord Samuel Spencer, MD. She stuck his card in her purse. Lucy gained her composure. She rolled her window up and then exited the car. The man asked Lucy her name. She told him. He asked what movie she was going to see. Lucy told him that she was at the movies with her children. He looked at her curiously. She explained that they were twelve. Dr. Spencer told her that she could call him anytime if she needed someone to talk with. Lucy again thanked him for his kindness. Dr. Spencer opened the door and Lucy walked in. Dr. Spencer shook her hand before they parted.

She returned to the movie theater that the children were in. The movie was at the end. The children got up. The three of them walked out of the theater. Lucy noticed Dr. Spencer at the ticket booth looking at them. They walked out of the theater. The children talked and laughed about the movie. The children chatted all the way home.

As the children talked amongst themselves Lucy thought about her conversation with Dr. Spencer. She was in deep thought. The children called her. Just as she was about to pass their street Lucy concentration was broken in time to turn onto her street. The children laughed. She pulled into the driveway. The children got out of the car and then called out to her. Lucy got out of the car and then walked to the front door. She opened it and the children ran in. They ran up to their rooms.

Lucy called her doctor and made an appointment to go in. She went into the kitchen and began dinner. Lucy tried not to alarm the children. She tried to act as normal as possible. She was happy when it was time for the children to go to bed.

She was exhausted from trying to keep up pretences. Lucy readied herself for bed. She laid awake thinking of the night before. Lucy laid in her bed wondering how a friend could do what Constance did. She couldn't understand why they targeted her. Lucy felt disgust and hate. Lucy prayed asking God to help her to get through this. Pure exhaustion finally took over and Lucy fell asleep. Lucy slept throughout the night.

The next morning she got up. Lucy prepared breakfast for the children. She called up to them. The children awakened and got ready for school. They ran downstairs and into the kitchen. The children quickly ate……………..

Lucy dropped them off and then returned home. She went up to her room and laid down. Lucy was happy to finally be alone. She was exhausted from putting up a front for her children. Lucy laid there thinking of what Dr. Lord Samuel Spencer said to her. She looked at the clock. It was too early to call into her doctor's office. Lucy closed her eyes and tried to clear her mind………………

Soon after she fell asleep……………………………..

It hadn't been long when Lucy was awakened by the buzzing of her cell phone. Lucy sluggishly reached for her phone, not bothering to look at the number.

"Hello."

"Hey Lucy. Are you ok?"

"Who is this?"

"Ruth. Did I wake you?"

"Yes."

"Lucy are you alright?"

"Yes. Why?"

"I heard."

"What did you hear?"

"Constance called me crying. She is all broken up."

"Really?"

"She told me about what they did to you and then right after leaving you they went to another one of her friend's homes and did the same thing to her. The girl fought and got hurt. She's in the hospital now. Lucy."

"Yeah."

"That dirty nasty so and so had sex with her with her passed out on the floor. Constance said that she tried to stop him once Sue, that is the girl's name, was unconscious, but he said that at least she stopped moving. Lucy she said that he did so many things to her. She said that if Sue had been awake she would have been screaming. Constance couldn't take it anymore. She eased out of the girl's bedroom and called the police. She guest he heard the sirens, because by the time the police came he had dressed and pretended that he was trying to wake her up by calling her baby and darling. The police at first was falling for it until they got a better look at the room and then began asking questions."

"What did Constance say?"

"She just cried, so they didn't think that she was involved."

"What's wrong with her?"

"She said that she's in love with him."

"But what they're doing is crazy."

"I told her that. Are you alright?"

"I'm handling it."

"Are you going to press charges?"

"I didn't plan to. I don't want to go through what I went through again, with them asking questions and then I would have to relive it."

"Well I'm not going to keep you. I didn't mean to wake you. I just wanted to make sure you were okay. Get some rest. If you need anything call me."

"Thank you for calling."

After Lucy hung up the phone she looked at the time. She saw that it was 10:30. She dialed her doctor's number. When the receptionist answered the phone Lucy gave her name and told the man that she needed to get in to see the doctor. She told him it was an emergency.

After a few minutes of silence the receptionist told her to come right in. Lucy thanked him and then hung up. She put on her shoes, brushed her teeth and then left.

As she drove to the doctor Lucy tried to stay calm and not worry. Lucy thought of her children and how she could not get sick. She thought of Jonathan, how she missed him and because he's not there who would take care of the children. Tears formed in her eyes. She thought of calling Ruth, but decided not to. Lucy felt alone............

She finally arrived at the medical facility. Lucy parked her car and then walked into the building. She walked into her doctor's office and gave her name. The receptionist told her to have a seat. Lucy picked up a magazine. She tried to concentrate on the article before her, but was unable to. Lucy happened to look up. Standing next to the receptionist was a man she thought looked familiar. Lucy tried not to stare, but she was trying to place where she knew the man. He happened to turn and catch her looking. Evidently he remembered her. He smiled and said hello. Lucy spoke and then out of the blue it hit her. She became embarrassed. His expression changed exhibiting a comforting look. The receptionist asked the doctor a question, which made him look away. Lucy was happy for the interruption. She looked back into the magazine afraid to look up.

A few minutes later Lucy's name was called. She got up. Lucy was led to an examining room. Her vitals were taken and she was instructed to remove the lower half of her clothes. The nurse left the room. Lucy removed her clothes and waited anxiously for the doctor to come in.

After what seemed to be an eternity the doctor walked into the office. He spoke and then asked her to lean back. While examining her the doctor asked Lucy a series of questions about why she was there. Lucy explained her reason. The doctor ordered culture to be done.

After his examination he placed his hand on her shoulder to console her. He reassured her that she had done the right thing by coming in right away. The doctor told her he didn't see anything and would rush the test. Lucy thanked him and then the doctor left the room. She quickly dressed and left the room.

As she walked towards the exit Lucy felt eyes on her. She turned and saw Dr. Spencer. He smiled at Lucy broadly and told her it was good seeing her. Lucy remained silent, not knowing what to say. He wished her well and she left the office. Lucy walked to her car. She looked at the time and realized it was almost time for the children to get out of school. She drove to their school and parked. Lucy became stressed thinking of what she would do if she had a terminal illness.

She could not think of an alternative so Lucy was determined to stay well enough to raise her children herself.

Lucy thoughts were interrupted by a tap on her window. She looked. It was her children. Lucy unlocked the door. The children got in. They excitedly chatted about school. Lucy had to stop them a few times to give each one a chance to get their story out and for her to understand what they were saying. The children kept Lucy from thinking of her problems…………………...

When they arrived home the children peeled out of the car. The family went into the house. They went up to their rooms to do their homework. Lucy prepared dinner. When it was done the children came down to the kitchen. The family sat and ate together. While eating JJ mentioned that Lucy looked sad. Joanna scolded him saying that she missed their father. Lucy did not correct them. When they were finshed eating the children returned to their rooms. Lucy cleaned the kitchen...................................

After she was done Lucy went to check on the children and then went to her room. Lucy changed her clothes and got into bed. She didn't spend any time thinking about her ordeal. Lucy went right to sleep..........................

By the end of the week Lucy had become anxious of not hearing from her doctor. She called the office. The receptionist told her that her doctor was out, but his partner was there. Lucy asked if he could have the doctor check and see if her results were in. The receptionist put her on hold. A few minutes went by. The receptionist returned to the phone. He informed Lucy that the doctor would like her to come in as soon as possible. Lucy's heart dropped. She told him that she would be there in a half hour. Lucy left the house and jumped into her car.

As she drove Lucy became nervous. She wondered what horrible disease she had contracted. She couldn't imagine the office wanting her to come in if nothing was there. Lucy began coaching herself to be calm and handle whatever news they had for her without falling apart..

When Lucy pulled into the parking area of the doctor's office she parked her car and then prayed. She sat there a few minutes to gain courage and then got out of her car. Lucy slowly walked towards the building. It seemed as if she was walking in slow motion and the building was further than she remembered. When she reached the building Lucy's hand trembled as she reached for the door handle. Lucy managed to open the door. She entered the building and then walked down the hall to the doctor's office. Lucy opened the door and then walked in. The office was empty. The receptionist took her name and told her to wait at the desk. He went to the back of the office. When he returned he opened the door and told Lucy to follow him. She did as she was told. The receptionist told Lucy to have a seat. As she sat in the examining room Lucy held her hands together trying to hold her composure. She had not been in the office, but a few minutes when the door opened. She looked up. Dr. Spencer walked into the room. He spoke and then sat on the stool in front of Lucy. In a calming voice he told her the results of the test. As he read each result Lucy quietly thanked God for it being negative. He then told her that she had been infected with Gonorrhea. Lucy's eyes began to water. The doctor told her that it was good that she came to the office as soon as she did. He told her that it was in its early stage and that he was going to give her a shot. He instructed her not to have intercourse for a period of time. Lucy didn't realize until after she had said, "There's no chance of that." Lucy realized how she must have sounded.

He looked at her curiously, but did not inquire. He knew this was not the place or time for questioning her about being attached. Dr. Spencer asked her to lower her pants. He gave her a shot of penicillin in her behind. She was instructed to get dress and come into his office. Lucy dressed and then went to Dr. Spencer's office. He stood up when she entered. He told her to have a seat and closed the door. He sat down. Dr. Spencer explained to her about HIV and AIDS. He encouraged her to follow up and return to take the test in 6 months. He said in a soothing voice not to worry. She thanked him for his time and then left his office. Lucy thanked God and prayed for protection. Lucy was somewhat relieved. She got into her car and drove home....

Chapter 8

Six months went by and Lucy returned to the doctor's office. As she was walking towards the building Lucy heard a car horn blow. Lucy looked. The car window opened. Lucy saw that it was Dr. Spencer. He smiled at her and spoke. She returned his greeting. He pulled over and got out of the car. He walked over to Lucy. The doctor asked for her forgiveness if she thinks him inappropriate, but he didn't know when there would be a better time. Dr. Spencer asked if they could go out some time. Lucy looked at him surprised and answered that she was married. The doctor again asked for her forgiveness and then went on to ask hadn't he been missing. Lucy thought about his question a few minutes. She asked if he had a pen. He took one out of his pocket and handed it to her. She took a receipt out of her purse and wrote her number on it and handed it to him. After handing it to Dr. Spencer Lucy commented that she wasn't promising anything. Dr. Spencer said fair enough. Lucy entered the building and walked down the hall. She entered the doctor's office. The receptionist spoke to her and told her to come right in. He buzzed her in. Lucy gave a blood sample and then left. She thanked the receptionist. Lucy got into her car. As Lucy drove home she thought of her giving Dr. Spencer her number. She began doubting her decision, feeling guilty that she was betraying her husband.....

Jonathan had been constantly reminded by Sally that she wanted to be with him and it had been eleven years. She expressed to him that if there had been someone back home they had probably moved on. Jonathan knew more than anyone how long it had been. He held back thinking of Lovely Lucy. He knew in his heart that she was special. He tried to explain this to Sally.

For years she had tried to understand and be patient. Sally began to press Jonathan asking him how long they would have to hold back their feelings. Jonathan thought of the questions she asked and knew that there had been many nights and mornings that he could have used a warm body. Jonathan apologized. It was getting late so he excused himself and went to bed. Jonathan laid in bed thinking about his dilemma and how he hated making Sally feel bad. Jonathan often asked himself how could he move on when he knew deep within that his heart belonged to someone else............................

It wasn't long before Jonathan fell asleep.

He began to dream: *Jonathan had begun having a recurring dream where he was on the beach making love to Lovely Lucy. He was now able to see her face. Jonathan thought her very beautiful. He held her face in his hands. They kissed passionately. He caressed her body. Jonathan loved the way she felt. For the first time he heard her speak. She told him how much she loved him. He could hear her moan as they made love. He held her tight never wanting to let her go. Jonathan whispered that he loved her and then laid back......*

The next morning Jonathan awakened. He saw the bed disheveled. Jonathan looked down and then cursed thinking how he had done it again. He got up and went into the bathroom. As he showered Jonathan thought how he had to stop. He remembered how vivid the dreams had become and knew that he would remember where he's from. Jonathan knew that he had to stay true and hold out. He returned to his room and dressed.....

A month went by. Sally began talking about them taking a vacation together. Curious Jonathan asked what she had in mind. She threw out some places, such as Jamaica, New Jersey, Atlantic City, Vegas and some others that became incoherent. He became dizzy. Jonathan excused himself and went to lay down.........................

Later that night Sally knocked on the door. He answered. Sally peeped her head in and asked if he was alright. Jonathan told her that he was fine and apologized if he alarmed her. She told him that she understood and not to worry about it. Sally said good night and then left his room..............

Five months had passed Sally prepared a special dinner. Jonathan asked her what was the occasion. Sally told Jonathan that she would tell him at dinner.

When they sat down to eat Sally fixed their plates. Jonathan began eating. He complimented her on the meal. Sally smiled. Jonathan noticed her mood was more up beat. He looked at Sally and asked what was going on. He thought maybe she had met someone. Sally was quiet for a few minutes and then she held her hands over the table for him to take. Reluctantly Jonathan took her hands. She looked into his eyes and told him that they were going to have a baby. Jonathan snatched his hands away. He stared at her. Then he asked what she meant. She told him that they had made love a few times. Jonathan looked confused, trying to remember. He couldn't recall any of the times. He expressed this. She informed him of her coming into his room on several occasions while he was asleep. She had gotten into bed with him and he had made love to her. He continued to stare at her. Sally said that she would leave before he awakened in the morning. Jonathan stood up exclaiming that it couldn't be true. All of a sudden he became dizzy. She went to his side. He asked her to move away from him. Jonathan managed to make it to his room. He locked the door behind himself. Sally knocked on his door. Jonathan told her to go away. She tried the handle.

After trying a few times to get him to open the door and him refusing Sally finally gave up and walked away. Sally returned to the kitchen with tears in her eyes. She began cleaning the kitchen. It was difficult to see the dishes because of the tears in her eyes. When she was finished cleaning the kitchen Sally returned to Jonathan's room. She knocked but there wasn't any answer.

"Jonathan please talk to me. I just wanted to be close to you. You would only love me when you slept. Jonathan I'm going to have your baby. You had to love me for me to get pregnant. Please talk to me. I'm six months."

Sally stopped talking, but continued to stand by the door…………………..

Jonathan laid in bed. His head was foggy. He heard Sally at his door. Jonathan couldn't believe what she had just told him. He felt as if his world had just caved in on him. He thought, "How can I be having a child with this woman? How could I have had sex with her and not known it? Why would she do this? I thought I could trust her to honor my feelings and situation." He was angry. He couldn't talk to her now………………

After some time Jonathan drifted off to sleep............................

The next morning Jonathan woke up. He felt different. As if it was new he sat up and looked around the room. He got up and walked to the door. When Jonathan opened the door he saw Sally sitting on the floor, asleep against the wall. Jonathan bent down and picked Sally up. She wrapped her arms around his neck. Jonathan carried Sally to her room. He gently placed her onto the bed. She kept her arms around his neck. Jonathan gently removed them. He kissed her on the forehead and then stood up straight. He looked around the room and spotted a chair. Jonathan walked over to it and moved it close to Sally's bed. Jonathan sat on it.

"Sally I know now this was a bad idea for me to have stayed here. I'm sorry for hurting you. This is what I was afraid of. Sally I know who I am now and where I'm from." Sally sat up. She had a look of fear on her face. "I'm so sorry. Sally I have a wife." Sally watched Jonathan. She watched as if a light went on inside of him.

"How do you know she hasn't moved on?"

"I have to take that chance. I love her as if it was yesterday that we met. I have a child, twins, they should be almost twelve now." Tears filled up in Sally's eyes. "I will stay until you have the baby, but then I have to leave. I will take care of the child and reimburse you for me staying here."

"How are you going to do that?"

"I will send you money and we can set up a visitation schedule."

"That won't work."

"Sally I have to return to my family. I have to go home."

"You are home. We can have a beautiful home here with our child."

"This is not my home. (He smoothed his hand along the side of her face.) I can't stay. I'm sorry, but I am not in love with you. I'm grateful for you taking me in when I needed somewhere to stay."

Sally began to cry. He sat on her bed and held her. After some time Sally fell asleep. Jonathan laid her down and left the room. He went into the bathroom and took a shower. While he took a shower everything came flooding back to him. He became dizzy and then leaned against the shower to keep from falling. He recalled the nights that Sally must have come into his room. Those were the nights that Jonathan thought he actually felt Lucy. Fear came over him. He wondered how she was doing. He wondered if she had in fact moved on...................

Lucy hired someone to stay with the twins while she go out on a date with Dr. Spencer. They had gone out to lunch a few times. He had finally convinced her to go out to dinner with him. She still had not spoken about him to the twins. Lucy didn't want to upset them. She still felt guilty, but felt the need for companionship. She no longer talked to any of her friends. Lucy did not trust to confide in Ruth because she still communicated with Constance. The last she had heard Constance was going to testify against Paul and had plea-bargained that she would get probation with intensive supervision. Lucy no longer wanted anything to do with anyone who had a relationship with Constance.

Lucy kissed her children good night. She gave the baby sitter instructions and left.

She drove to a restaurant outside of town. Lucy didn't want to run into anyone she knew. She wasn't ready for the obvious questions. Lucy arrived early. She walked into the restaurant. Lucy was immediately seated. Lucy told the waiter that she had a guest coming. The waiter asked if she would like to order something to drink. She ordered soda. While Lucy waited for Dr. Spencer she sat and sipped on her drink. She thought of her life up until this moment. Here she sat waiting for a man who was not her husband. She asked herself if this was scandalist.

Lucy noticed Dr. Spencer walking towards the table. He gave her one of his bright smiles. When he made it to the table Dr. Spencer leaned over and lightly kissed her on the side of her face.

It had been six months since they had begun going out and Lucy could tell he wanted to be closer. She admitted to herself that he had come along at a time when she needed someone strong. He had helped Lucy through her emotional state………

Dr. Spencer broke her concentration. He made light conversation……………..

As they ate Lucy noticed the way Dr. Spencer looked at her. She tried not to look at him. After they finished eating Dr. Spencer took her hand. He looked very serious. He reached into his pocket and took out a box. He placed the box on the table. Lucy looked at the box. He took her hand and with his free hand opened the box. Lucy looked at it. She thought it beautiful. It was platinum with one-carat diamond, surrounded by another carat of diamonds. He moved the ring close to Lucy and then asked if she would marry him.

Lucy blurted out, "But I'm already married."

Lucy showed him the ring that she was still wearing.

Dr. Spencer insisted that she had been a good wife and no longer needed to wait for a man who was never coming back. He went on to say that legally she could be considered a widow. The look that she gave Dr. Spencer made him realize that he had said the wrong thing. He tried to apologize. She stood up. Lucy through glassy eyes looked at Dr. Spencer and thanked him for the dinner. She apologized and said she had to leave.

Dr. Spencer waved the waiter over and asked for the check. He watched as Lucy exited the restaurant. When the waiter returned Dr. Spencer quickly gave the waiter cash and told him to keep the change.

The waiter looked at the money and then yelled thanks.

Dr. Spencer quickly ran out of the restaurant. Lucy was backing out. Dr. Spencer ran to the driver side of her car. He yelled out I'm sorry. Lucy felt for him, but she couldn't talk to him right now. She put the car in drive and continued out of the parking lot. She could barely see the road for the tears running down her eyes. She managed to make it home. Lucy pulled down her visor and looked at her face. She found Kleenex in her purse. She wiped her face. Lucy didn't want the sitter asking if she was alright. When Lucy thought that she had hidden her feelings she got out of her car and headed into the house. She had the money ready to pay the sitter. When she entered the house the sitter was in the family room. Lucy paid the sitter and thanked her. She walked the sitter to the front door. The sitter said thank you and then left. Lucy watched as the sitter got into her car and drove away.

She went back into the house and locked her front door. Lucy's cell phone began vibrating. She ignored it, knowing it was Dr. Spencer. Lucy made sure her house was locked and looked in on her children. She then went into her room................

For the next six months Lucy refused Dr. Spencer's calls. She realized that it wasn't what he said, she just wasn't ready to move on. She knew it might seem silly, but Lucy believed that Jonathan was alive and until she felt differently she would be patient and wait........................

Jonathan promised Sally that he would stay until the baby was born, but then would return home to his wife. He told Sally that he was grateful for all that she had done for him, but he loved his wife and children.

When he was alone Jonathan smiled wondering how they look. He wondered what she had.

As time passed Sally began thinking that she didn't want to keep the baby. She discussed this with Jonathan. Jonathan didn't believe what he was hearing. He told her that he wouldn't be able to live with himself giving his child up, but Sally was determined that she couldn't bare seeing his child everyday and he not be there. Jonathan sat quiet for a while thinking about his situation. His mind went to Lucy. He wondered how she was dealing with his absence. Jonathan then thought of his position with Sally. He tried to be calm. Jonathan thought, "How can Sally have come into his room and now that reality has come to play want to get rid of a child she is carrying?" Jonathan tried to understand because he knew that he didn't make things easier by staying with her. He accepted blame because deep down Jonathan knew that he had in some way led her on.................

By the time Sally was to deliver they decided that Jonathan would take the child back with him.

Jonathan called Raymond. At first Raymond didn't believe it was him. As Jonathan continued talking to Raymond tears filled his eyes. Raymond filled Jonathan in on Lucy and the twins. That is as much or as little as he knew. He hadn't been around them in the past two years so he didn't know what had been going on in her life, or what she was going through. Jonathan filled his friend in on his situation. Raymond remained quiet. Jonathan asked Raymond to purchase a ticket for him. He asked Raymond not to tell Lucy about him being alive and coming home. He told Raymond that he would be ready to leave as soon as the baby was born. He asked Raymond to promise that he would keep everything to himself. Raymond promised his friend that he would.

After hanging up the phone Jonathan thought how wonderful it was that Lucy had not moved on. He thought if it was possible this made his love for her grow even more. Then he thought how awful it must have been for her holding on when everything and everyone told her that she wasn't being realistic……………..…

After getting off of the phone Raymond called Lucy. She was happy to hear from him. He was the closes thing other than the children she had of Jonathan's. They talked for an hour. When she got off the phone Lucy felt happier than she had in a while. Lucy couldn't believe that in just a few words he had given her new hope. She didn't feel stupid for believing that one day her husband would return to her.

Lucy called Dr. Spencer. He sounded happy to hear from her. She broke the news to him that it was useless for them to go on. Dr. Spencer tried to change her mind. She told him it was no use that she wasn't ready to give up on Jonathan. She thanked him for his helping her to get through some difficult times and apologized for leading him on. Dr. Spencer accepted Lucy's decision and told her if she happens to change her mind look him up. They talked a few minutes longer with Dr. Spencer telling her how wonderful she was and then they hung up.....................................

Sally came and knocked on Jonathan's door. She informed him that it was time. Jonathan thought of Lucy. He began to think of how lonely it must have been for Lucy to not have him by her side when it came time to deliver the twins. As Sally breathed and pushed Jonathan wondered if Lucy had any complications. He wondered if she had a rough time. He felt bad that all he could think of while Sally carried and now that she was about to deliver his child was Lucy. Jonathan made sure that he was supportive and she was comfortable.

When the baby was out tears formed in his eyes. The doctor held his baby girl up to him. He thought that she was the most beautiful baby he had ever seen.

After holding the baby up the nurse took her away. Jonathan kissed Sally on the forehead. Sally was taken to her room. She seemed sad. Jonathan understood this, but he couldn't stay with her. He also reasoned that he never promised her anything, didn't lead her on and heck as far as he was concerned hadn't technically had sex with her. He was under the impression that it was Lucy he was making love to and he had dreamed it..........

The next day Sally was released. Jonathan gathered what few clothes he had and the few things for the baby together.

When they got to the airport Sally reassured the staff that she had given Jonathan the okay to take their daughter. Jonathan asked Sally if she wanted a moment alone with the baby. Sally declined, saying that it was better that way. She put on a brave face. She assured Jonathan that her decision was best. He walked to the gate glancing back once. He felt bad for her and hoped that she would find a man to love her. He thought how she had her whole life ahead of her. She was at least ten years younger than he.

As he sat waiting for his flight a pilot walked up to him. The pilot excused himself and hesitantly asked if he was Jonathan Mills. Jonathan stood up. He smiled, repositioned the bundle in his arms and then held his hand out. The man was taken aback. He shook Jonathan's hand and hugged him. He asked Jonathan was he on his flight. He looked at Jonathan's ticket and saw that he was. The pilot continued to hold Jonathan's hand and placed his free hand behind Jonathan's back and told him to come with him. The pilot saw that it was an open seat in first class and put Jonathan in it. He then asked Jonathan whose baby he was holding. Jonathan told him it was a long story. The pilot smiled and said we have time. The co-pilot came into the plane. Jonathan was in the cot-pit. They stopped talking when he entered. The pilot introduced him to Jonathan. Jonathan shook the man's hand. He explained who Jonathan was. The man looked shocked. The pilot asked if Jonathan mind talking in front of the co-pilot. Jonathan told him that he didn't mind. So Jonathan continued with his story. The men listened intently..............

When Jonathan was finished the men inquired asking what he would do if his wife didn't accept the baby. Jonathan had not thought of that. He looked down at his sleeping baby girl. He thought how tiny she was. He loved her even though he had only known her for a few hours. Jonathan looked back up at the men and confided that he had not thought that far out. The pilot reassured Jonathan that Lucy would be so happy with his return that she would accept the baby. The men then changed the subject. They talked of lighter matters......

When the plane touched down Jonathan became nervous. He wondered if Lucy still loved him and if she would accept him not to mention the baby. Jonathan shook the pilot's hand and then left the plane. He walked through the gate and once he made it to the end of the gate he immediately spotted his friend. His friend smiled broadly and fought back tears. He walked quickly to him. He shook his hand and then hugged his best friend. Raymond looked at the baby and told him that she looked like Joanna. Jonathan looked at Raymond with glassy eyes. Raymond realized that he had not mentioned the twin's names. Jonathan smiled as Raymond told him that Lucy had named the children after him. His daughter was Joanna Christina and son JJ short for Jonathan Christian Jr. Jonathan smiled broadly. During their ride Raymond filled Jonathan in on what he had been doing with his life...................

Raymond called Lucy to see if she was home. She was. He asked if she was alone. Lucy told him that the children were in school. Raymond told her that he was on his way to see her. She told him that was fine. She told him that she would make them breakfast. He told her fine and that he would see her soon. The two hung up.......................

Raymond informed Jonathan of such. Jonathan was happy that she was alone so they could talk and discuss the baby. Raymond noticed that Jonathan had become nervous. He reassured Jonathan that things would work out............................

A half hour later Raymond pulled up in front of Lucy's home. Jonathan asked whose house it was. Raymond had forgotten to tell him that she had purchased a home and moved. Jonathan looked at Raymond and said, "You forgot to tell me a lot."

Jonathan got out of the car. He shook Raymond's hand and thanked him. Jonathan took his bag and his baby out of the car and walked up to the door. He rang the doorbell. A few minutes later the door opened. Raymond sat looking on. At first Lucy stared at Jonathan in disbelief. Her eyes became teary. Raymond smiled as he saw arms wrap around his friend's neck. Raymond beeped the horn. Both Jonathan and Lucy looked and waved. They walked into the house.

Once inside Lucy noticed that Jonathan was holding something. She looked down and realized it was a baby. She moved back. Jonathan noticed the confused look wash over her face. He started by saying it's a long story. Lucy asked if he was hungry. He said that he was. She led him into the kitchen. The baby began squirming. Lucy asked if she was hungry. Jonathan told her that he had milk in his bag. He went to get it. Lucy watched him. She couldn't believe that it was Jonathan.

When he took the bottle out Lucy took the baby from him and told him to sit and eat. He had lost a lot of weight. She asked if he was well. He joked saying that he missed her cooking. Lucy looked at the baby and saw how she looked like the twins. She began feeding the baby. Jonathan took a bite and then said how good it was being back and how much he missed her. He felt nervous.

When he said nothing more Lucy interrupted his thoughts and asked what's the story. Jonathan began to tell Lucy his ordeal. As he ate his meal, with every bite memories flashed before him. Lucy waited patiently listening to every word. Jonathan and the baby had finished eating before he was finished telling his story. Lucy placed the baby to her chest, thinking this baby was a part of Jonathan. They moved into the den. She laid the baby on the couch next to her. Jonathan wanted so much to hold Lucy, but resisted the temptation.

He wasn't sure where they stood and didn't want to rush her into anything that she may not be ready for.

When he had finished his story of twelve years away from her tears were running down Lucy's cheeks. He could no longer resist. Jonathan walked over to Lucy and took her into his arms. He felt so good. Her tears wet his shirt. Jonathan lifted her chin. He began kissing her. He pulled her close. Lucy remembered this familiar feeling. She could feel that he wanted her. Lucy stopped and moved back. Jonathan looked at her curious.

Lucy told him that she had her own twelve years of story. Jonathan sat back. He listened intently. There were a few times when she saw anger. She also saw a gentleness and comforting look. When she was done he brought her into his arms and held her. He kissed her neck, sending shivers throughout her body. The baby moved.

Lucy pulled away and picked the baby up. Lucy asked what was the baby's name. Jonathan asked if she could accept the baby. She looked down at the baby and saw Jonathan's smile on her face. When Lucy said that she could Jonathan took out a form from his bag. The baby hadn't been named and parents weren't on the form. Lucy looked at him after seeing the form. He asked Lucy would she be the child's mother. She asked if he was sure. Lucy looked into Jonathan's eyes and saw the fear in them. She nervously took the paper, walked over to the desk and signed her name in the mother's space. They decided to name the baby Joann Christie. After filling out the form he folded, placed it in an envelope and put it in the mailbox out side of the house.

Lucy told him that it was time to pick up the children. He told her that he would stay home and wait for them to return. Lucy informed him that she had kept all of the children baby things. She told him where to find them and that they could convert one of the guest bedrooms to be a nursery for Joann. Jonathan took her into his arms and asked if she was sure about all of this. She smoothed her hand over his cheek and said yes. He took her hand and kissed it. She told him she had to leave. She lightly kissed him and then left.

After she left Jonathan looked around the first floor. Then he went upstairs and looked in each room. He touched a few things in his son's room, smiling at the thought of having a son. When he went into his oldest daughter's room he smiled looking at a picture of her on the dresser. He lifted Joann up and thought how she did look like her older sister. He left her room. He looked in the first guest room and asked if Joann liked it. She didn't make a sound. Then he went into the next guest room and looked around. Again he asked Joann about that one as well. He thought maybe. He finally made it down to the last bedroom, which was the master suite. He entered a small hallway, which led into the bathroom. He thought it huge. Then he continued to where there was an opening. He walked through the opening, which led to the bedroom. He smiled thinking how Lucy had kept some of his things. Jonathan felt more love for Lucy thinking of how she had kept him with her all these years. He remembered how he had once wondered when they were returning from their honeymoon whether Lucy would continue to love him. Looking around her bedroom he felt hope that they would be okay...........................

Lucy wondered if she could possible be dreaming. She felt an overwhelming feeling to cry. She tried to hold back the tears. Lucy wiped her eyes continuously. She could barely see. As she pulled up to the curb Lucy pulled down her visor. She looked into it. Lucy looked into her purse and pulled out Kleenex. She wiped her face and again managed to hide her emotions. When the children entered the car they spoke and as usual talked of their day. They did not pickup on Lucy's emotions.............................

As Jonathan continued to look around the room he thought the new things worked well with the old. Jonathan left the bedroom and then went down to the basement. He admired the theater and imagined the children playing in the rec room. He then spotted the sofa and an image flashed before his eyes of Lucy being pinned down struggling. Jonathan became angry. He thought of how it never would have happened if he had been there. He continued toward the back of the basement. He went through a door. There he saw the baby things. He looked them over and tried to imagine his children when they were babies. He heard something upstairs and wondered if it was his family. A flood of feelings came rushing over him...

Jonathan started up the stairs. When he got up to the top Jonathan heard the children. Jonathan closed the basement door and followed the chatter. When he walked into the kitchen the children turned and looked. They stopped talking. Lucy went over to Jonathan and took the baby. She smiled up at Jonathan and then told the children that he was their father. They looked at Lucy and then at Jonathan. Joanna walked over to him, gave him a quick hug and said hi. She moved and then J.J. walked over and held his hand out. Jonathan shook it. J.J. also quickly moved back. The children just stared at their father. They looked back at Lucy. Joanna asked who the baby was. Lucy looked down at the baby and smiled. She looked at her children and said that she was their baby sister. They looked at her curiously. Lucy told them that God blessed them with this precious baby girl. The children walked over to Lucy and looked at the baby. Joanna asked how she could be their sister. Lucy looked at Jonathan and said daddy made her. The children didn't understand. Joann began moving. Lucy got a bottle and then sat down. The children stood next to her and watched in amazement as Lucy fed the baby. Lucy looked up at Jonathan. She asked him if he was tired. She told him to go up and take a warm shower. She informed him that his clothes were in his closet.

Jonathan walked out of the kitchen and went up to the bedroom. The first closet revealed Lucy's clothes. He closed it back and then looked in another closet and discovered all of his clothes.

At first he just stared at them. His eyes became watery. He couldn't believe she had waited for him and saved all of his clothes. He touched the clothes, actually missing them. He took out a pair of jeans. Jonathan opened a draw and found a shirt and looked in another finding a t-shirt, boxers and socks. The clothes were like old friends. They were familiar. He laid the clothes on the vanity chair in the bathroom. Jonathan found a washcloth and bath towel. He turned the water on in the shower. Jonathan took the clothes off that he had been wearing. He stepped into the shower and let the water run over him. He stuck his head under the water and then began washing himself. Jonathan washed as if he was trying to remove twelve years of himself being away. He placed the soap down and leaned his hands against the wall. He cried. Jonathan cried for the twelve years he was away from his wife, the twelve years he missed his kids being born and their growing up. He cried for the pain, ordeal his wife had to endure with his being gone and what she had to go through with the rape. He cried for the twelve years that he had lost with his wife. He cried for the twelve years that Sally lost out, maybe in finding someone to love her and giving up her first-born. He cried for not feeling anything for her and leaving her with nothing. Jonathan turned the water off and dried off. He put on his clothes and then laid down. He could smell the scent of Lucy's perfume. He soon drifted off to sleep...........................

Lucy laid Joann in Joanna's bed. They put pillows around her. Lucy and the children went into the second guest room and moved furniture around. They then went down to the basement and got some of Joanna baby's furniture and took it up to the guest room. Lucy washed the furniture and mattress. She put the baby covers in the wash. When they had finished drying Lucy placed them on the bed. She then took Joann out of Joanna's bed and placed her in the crib. Lucy placed cover over her and then smoothed her hand over the baby's back.

Lucy directed the children to do their homework and then she went down to the kitchen to start dinner. She returned to the basement and looked in a chest. There she took some of Joanna's baby clothes and put them in the wash. Lucy returned to the kitchen and continued preparing dinner. She then went up to her bedroom. Lucy smiled when she saw Jonathan laying on the bed. She stared at him a few minutes thinking of how long she had waited for this moment. Lucy eased out of her clothes and changed into lounging clothes. She eased out of the room.

Lucy returned to the kitchen and finished cooking. She set the dining room table. Just as Lucy was about to call the children to dinner J.J. and Joanna were coming downstairs. J.J. was carrying Joann. She was happy that the children had taken a liking to their sister. J.J. handed the baby to Lucy. She took the baby and went to get a bottle out of the refrigerator. She warmed the milk. Lucy told the children to sit at the dining room table. Before leaving the kitchen Joanna asked where was their father. Lucy gave the baby to J.J. and told him to finish feeding his sister, while she go wake their father. She smiled at the thought of Jonathan being upstairs. She had waited so long for this moment. Lucy left the kitchen and started up the stairs. She took each step constantly looking up. Lucy slowly walked down the hallway. When she made it to the end of the hallway Lucy slowly opened her bedroom door. When she entered the bedroom Lucy saw Jonathan still sleeping peacefully on her bed. She hated to disturb him. She slowly walked towards him not wanting to wake him. Lucy sat on the bed next to him. She bent down and kissed him lightly on the lips. She then whispered wake up. Jonathan stirred. She called his name out. Jonathan opened his eyes. When he saw her Jonathan smiled and then reached for her. He wrapped his arms around her and pulled Lucy to him. She laid there in his arms, feeling his strength, his love. Lucy took in his smell, remembering how much she loved it and missed it. Jonathan kissed her neck and then told her he was happy to be home. Lucy moved back. She looked into his eyes that stared back at her the way she once remembered.

"Are you real?"

"Yes. I'm sorry I didn't regain my memory sooner." Jonathan sat up. "You know even though I had lost my memory I remembered Lovely Lucy." Lucy smiled. "At first I couldn't see your face, but I was with you. Remember our honeymoon, on the beach?" Lucy covered her face. "I would go there in my dreams and then I finally saw your face. I also knew there was someone in my life I had to get back to." He put his finger under her chin. "I somehow knew there was someone that I had to remember and come home to."

Lucy wrapped her arms around Jonathan and hugged him.

"Did you ever have feelings for that woman you lived with? How old was she?"

Jonathan pulled her back and looked into her eyes.

"Lovely Lucy once you captured my heart there was no one else for me, even with my memory gone my heart remembered."

"But you had forgotten me."

"I never forgot about you. My heart never forgot about you. They told me that I called out your name."

"But." Lucy looked down.

"Sweet heart I know it's hard for you to believe what I told you, but it is the truth. She is thirty-five." He saw the expression on Lucy's face. "I never cheated on you and never will. I did not intentionally have sex with that woman. I truly was dreaming of you and had no idea. I thought that I was making love to you. I was surprised and disgusted with myself for this happening. I always told the woman that I knew there was someone else. I guest she had hopes that in time I would no longer have the feelings that I have for you. She didn't know that there would never be a time when I don't love you the way that I do. Please believe me."

"Yes." Lucy laid her head on Jonathan's chest. He held her firm. Jonathan knew Lucy wanted to believe him. He knew he would have to work to gain her trust. Their concentration was broken when they heard Joanna calling up to Lucy.

"I forgot. I came up to get you for dinner."

Lucy got up. She held her hand out to him. He took it and they walked down the hall. Lucy felt a comfort with her small hands in his large warm hands. As they walked down the hall Joanna watched her parents. She watched her mother. It seemed like she had never seen her mother look this way. It was like the sadness that she saw in her mother's eyes had vanished and commented on it. Lucy smoothed her hand over Joanna's face and then smiled at her.

When they had made it downstairs Jonathan smoothed his free hand over Joanna's head. Joanna looked up at her father and smiled. It warmed his heart. They walked into the dining room and saw J.J. sitting at the table playing with Joann. Jonathan was happy that the children seemed to be accepting their sister. He thought how he didn't know what he would do if they hadn't accepted her. Lucy took Joann from J.J. and laid her in a bassinet that she had brought into the dining room. Jonathan was seated at the head of the table. Lucy had them all take hands and she said a prayer. When she was done the family began to eat.

As they ate J.J. began asking his father about his ordeal. Lucy listened intently, feeling guilty for thinking Jonathan was enjoying himself. She sat watching her family mingle thinking how she had imagined it would be. She looked over at Joann. She had fallen asleep. When the children were finished eating they excused themselves. Jonathan and Lucy were left alone except for the sleeping infant close beside her. Jonathan smiled and complimented Lucy on the meal. He asked if the children were usually as chattery as they were at dinner. Lucy told him that they were. Lucy and Jonathan talked for an hour before she finally stood up and began clearing the table. Jonathan stood and began to help.

"You don't have to help. I know you're tired from your travel. Go up and get rest."

"Are you sure?"

"Yes. Go on."

"Do you want me to take the baby up?"

"No, she may get up again. You need to get your rest."

Jonathan walked over to Lucy. He placed his hands on each side of her face.

"You don't have to do this."

"I know. I want to. Go, you need your rest."

He leaned down and kissed her.

"Okay. If you need me let me know."

"I will."

Jonathan headed upstairs. He began walking down the hall towards Lucy's bedroom. Jonathan stopped at J.J.'s room. The door was open. Jonathan knocked. J.J. looked up. He told his father to come in. Jonathan entered the room, pulled up a chair and sat down. Jonathan asked J.J. about his likes and dislikes. At first J.J. was hesitant. J.J. seemed nervous. As Jonathan talked J.J. began to relax. J.J. showed him the assignment that he was working on and seemed impressed when his father was able to explain the assignment. Jonathan started feeling sluggish. He told J.J. that he would let him finish up. He kissed his son on the forehead and said good night.

Jonathan left the room and went a few feet where he stopped at Joanna's door and knocked. She said come in. Jonathan walked over to her. She was on the computer. He asked what she was doing. Joanna told him that she was talking with a friend. Jonathan asked if she had done her homework and she told him that she had. He leaned over and kissed her on the forehead. He told her good night and left her room. Jonathan closed the door.

As he began his walk down the hall again Jonathan stopped when something caught his eye. He peered into the room. He was amazed to see that many of the things for the nursery were in the room. Jonathan was feeling dizzy so he left the room and continued down the hall.

When he finally made it to Lucy's bedroom Jonathan took his clothes off. He pulled the covers back and layed down. It didn't take long before he fell asleep.

As he slept Jonathan began to dream: "*He was piloting the plane. Something went wrong. He tried to call in to let them know that he had to change course. They couldn't understand him. Jonathan tried to turn the plane around to get to the closes piece of land. The plane began to shake. He alerted his crew and then made an announcement. He continued trying to make it to land. Jonathan could see land far off as the plane descending through the clouds. He could hear screaming from outside of the cockpit. He made another announcement for everyone to stay calm and prepare themselves for a crash landing. The plane was desending quickly. He tried to release the landing gear, but it didn't work. He decided to land on the water to make a softer landing. They crashed into the ocean. Part of the plane flew close to the island and others further out into the ocean. The flight crew let down the emergency doors and began helping everyone out of the plane. The staff helped the people assemble their floating devices. Jonathan had been thrown away from the plane. He tried to swim to what he thought was land. He could not see very well because he had hit his head on something. He passed out. He could see himself floating. After some time someone came to his rescue and asked if he was alright. Jonathan could hear them working on him, but it seemed as if he had left his body. He could hear himself calling for Lovely Lucy…….*"

Lucy cleaned the dining room and then set the table. She washed up the dishes and cleaned the kitchen. Lucy put up the leftover food. She turned out the light. Lucy returned to the dining room and picked up Joann. Joann stirred. Lucy smoothed her hand over the baby's back. She turned out the dining room light. Lucy started upstairs. She walked slowly, trying not to disturb the sleeping baby. As she walked down the hall she stopped at J.J.'s room. She knocked. He told her to enter. She entered the room. Lucy kissed him on the side of his face and told him to go to bed. J.J. said good night. She then walked to Joanna's room and told her to go to bed. She kissed her daughter and then left the room. Lucy went into Joann's room and laid her in the crib. She smoothed her hand over her back and then left the room. Lucy left the door cracked.

She then headed to her bedroom. When she got to her bedroom Lucy went in. She saw that Jonathan was asleep. Lucy eased in the room and closed the door quietly. She went into the bathroom and closed the door. She didn't want to disturb Jonathan with the noise from the shower. Lucy removed her clothes and then turned on the shower. Lucy let the warm water run over her body. It had been a long day. Lucy let the warmth of the water wash over her body. She then began washing her body and then rinsed off. Lucy dried off and then put on a nightgown. She eased into the room and became alarmed when she saw Jonathan moaning. She thought he was sick. Lucy rushed over to him and realized he was having a nightmare. Lucy smoothed her hand over the side of his face. She called out his name softly. She continued calling his name until he awakened. He opened his eyes and just stared at her. She asked if he was alright. He continued to stare. Lucy asked him again if he was alright. Jonathan realized where he was and took her into his arms. He held her asking if she was really real. Lucy kissed him on the lips. She then moved back and told him that he was home.

Jonathan laid back. She laid her head on his chest. When he fell back to sleep Lucy tried to turn without disturbing him. Although she was exhausted Lucy couldn't get to sleep. She laid in bed trying to clear her mind. There was so much going through her head. Thinking of the days' events and now it being quiet in the house everything began running through her head. She felt the warmth from Jonathan's body and thought of how many nights she layed in bed thinking about him being there, wanting and needing him to be there. She lay there for hours trying to get the fact of his closeness from her mind and let sleep take over. Lucy felt an arm wrap around her waist. Jonathan pulled her closer to him. He whispered that he missed being close to her. Lucy caressed his arm. Jonathan kissed her neck. She placed her hand on the back of his head. He turned her around. He laid on his side. Jonathan pulled the covers back.

"What are you doing?"

"I want to look at my wife. Am I really here?"

"I've gotten older."

"You're still the beautiful, vibrant woman I met seems like just a year for me. You know we were not even married for a year before...."

"I know."

"I'm sorry we never got to celebrate our first wedding anniversary."

"It wasn't your fault."

"I just hate that we missed out on so many years."

"We will just have to make up for that."

"Lucy it's been a long time."

"I know."

"Can I?"

"Do you want to."

"Why wouldn't I?"

"Remember what I told you?"

"But you're healthy."

"Yes, but I didn't think after what happened to me you would want to touch me like before."

Jonathan sat up. He took Lucy by the shoulders.

"Are you kidding me? You are as beautiful as you were twelve years ago and your body look better than it did or what I remember when I first met you."

"I don't know about that. I have twelve years on me."

"You wear them well. Lovely Lucy I love you. You will look good when we're a hundred years old."

"Jonathan."

"Baby I know you've been hurt. I love you and you are a beautiful desirable woman."

Jonathan smoothed his hand down Lucy's face. He brought her face to his and kissed her. His kiss was gentle and sweeter than she'd remembered. He held this kiss savoring the moment. He smoothed his face against hers. His face was rough from him not shaving, but she didn't mind. Lucy had missed his touch, his smell, Jonathan's gentleness. He laid her back. Jonathan looked down at his wife and thought how beautiful she was. He laid next to her and caressed her body. Lucy trembled under his touch. Tears filled her eyes and ran down her face. When he kissed her lips Jonathan taste the salt from the tears. He looked at her. He asked if she was alright. Lucy whispered that she had stopped believing he would return to her. Jonathan kissed each eye and said sweet. He then kissed her lips. It was gentle and then became passionate. Lucy was lost in his passion. Jonathan took his time wanting to savor this moment. He paused and looked down at her. She looked up at him. She saw the hesitation. She knew where it was coming from. Lucy brought her hands to his face. "It's me. You're really home." Jonathan kissed her again and then they were lost..............................

At five a.m. Lucy heard a faint cry. At first she was dazed. Then Lucy remembered the baby. She searched around in the dark for her slippers and housecoat. She finally found them and quietly left the room. Lucy walked down the hall. She picked up her pace. Joann was screaming and shaking by the time Lucy entered the room. She rocked her and talked to Joann as she walked down the hall. Lucy walked down the stairs and to the kitchen. Once in the kitchen Lucy began singing to the baby. She reached into the refrigerator and took milk out. She noticed that it was running low. Lucy told Joann that she was going to have to get her some more milk. Joann sniffled and looked at Lucy with eyes full of tears, but it seemed like she understood. Lucy warmed the bottle. When it was warm enough she carried Joann into the den. She sat in the rocking chair and began feeding Joann. Lucy looked down at this beautiful baby. She wondered how her mother could have given her away. She wondered what she was thinking. Lucy wondered what the baby's mother looked like and would she return one day looking for her child. She wondered if Jonathan felt anything for the woman. Lucy knew what he told her, but deep down thought maybe there had been something there. She did not think that he intentionally sought the woman out, but they had spent twelve years together. Twelve of their years they missed.

After Joann had finished eating Lucy put the bottle down and placed the baby on her chest. Lucy rubbed Joann's back. Lucy thought back to when her children were babies. She kissed Joann on the head. The baby seemed relaxed in Lucy's arms. Lucy closed her eyes. Lucy soon drifted off to asleep.

At six o'clock Lucy heard her alarm clock go off. She jumped. Lucy realized that she was holding Joann. She rubbed her back, trying not to wake her. Lucy got up and headed upstairs. She continued to hold Joann. Lucy knocked on J.J.'s door and told him to get up. Then she went to Joanna's door and knocked on it. Joanna answered back saying she was up. Lucy went into Joann's room and washed her. She dressed the baby. Lucy went to her bedroom. Surprisingly Jonathan was awake. Lucy told Jonathan she was sorry about the alarm. He told her not to worry about it. He told her to come to him. She obeyed. When she was close Jonathan reached out and pulled her closer. He looked at Joann.

"I'm sorry I didn't hear her."

"Don't worry about it." Lucy looked down at Joann. "Me and this little lady is getting to know each other. She needs food and clothes."

"I have to get my I.D. I need to call my job."

"I'm sure they are not going to believe you survived. I bet they will be happy that I saved the money that they paid me for……. (Lucy's voice cracked)."

Jonathan took her hands and kissed them.

"I know."

"Do you?" Lucy couldn't finish the sentence.

"No. I am officially retired."

"I have to take the kids to school and then I'll go to the grocery store. Do you want me to take the baby?"

"No. You can leave her. I'll reach out to my job while you're out. By the way what did you do with my car?"

"In the garage. I drove it around the corner every so often so it would work when you returned."

Jonathan stood up. He kissed Lucy. They heard a knock on the door. Lucy told them to come in. As if the children were surprised to see their father they looked at their father a few minutes before speaking. Lucy told them to go down and get cereal and she would be right down. The children left the room. Lucy laid Joann on the bed and placed pillows around her. She went into the bathroom. She turned the shower on and then took her robe off. Just as she was about to step into the shower Jonathan took her hand. She had not heard him come in. Jonathan asked if he could join her. Lucy nodded yes. He removed his pants and followed her. Lucy picked up the Lufa, put shower gel on it and began lathering Jonathan's body.

"I miss this."

"Me too."

Jonathan took Lucy into his arms and kissed her. After a few minutes Lucy pulled away.

"We don't have time."

"Let me just hold you a little while."

Lucy looked into his eyes. She didn't want to deny this man anything, but she knew the children were waiting.

"The children."

Jonathan smiled and took the lufa from her. He poured shower gel on it and proceeded to go over Lucy's body with it. As he washed her body Lucy resisted the temptation to sub-come to his touch. His touch was maddening. When he was finished what he called cleaning her Lucy stood under the water to rinse off. The warm water didn't help what she was now feeling. She was aroused to the point it hurt, but Lucy reminded herself that the children were waiting. She stepped out of the shower, lightly kissed Jonathan and then grabbed the drying towel. She dried off and then went into the bedroom. Lucy grabbed some sweats and put them on. She put on a pair of sneakers and ran downstairs. She told the twins to come on and left out of the house. The children left out of the house. They got into the car.

As Lucy drove the children to school the children asked about their father. They were curious to know if he was going to stay. Lucy asked why did they ask that. J.J. told her that he thought his father was nice and wanted him to stay around. Joanna conferred this sentiment and added that she liked the way Lucy looked now. Lucy smiled to herself, happy that they had taken to their father……………..

She pulled up in front of the school. The children kissed Lucy and jumped out of the car. Lucy watched as the children went into the building. She pulled off. Lucy drove to the grocery store. She picked up several cases of baby formula, diapers, wipes and then went to the clothing area and then picked up a few baby sleepers. Lucy filled her cart with foods that she remembered Jonathan liked. She pushed the cart towards the register. She looked down at the food in the cart wondering if Jonathan still enjoyed these foods. She decided to purchase them anyway.

As Lucy continued to the register she thought of how she really didn't know a lot about her husband. Lucy laughed to herself thinking of all that they had already been through. She thought of how they had been married for twelve years, but hadn't known each other for very long and had only lived together for little more than six months.

When Lucy got to the register the cashier spoke. She was familiar with Lucy. The woman began scanning her grocery. As the woman scanned Lucy noticed the lady looked at the baby items and then looked at her. After she had finished scanning the grocery the woman asked about the baby things. Lucy smiled saying that the baby was three days old. The woman told Lucy that she looked good. Lucy again said thank you and paid for her grocery. The cashier told one of the male employees to help Lucy. She had never done it before, so Lucy presumed it was because the woman thought she had just had a baby. Lucy was grateful for the help.

When the grocery was loaded into the car Lucy headed home.....

When Lucy arrived home she began bringing the grocery in. As she stepped into the kitchen Lucy saw Jonathan. He asked what was she doing carrying grocery. Lucy explained that she was use to doing it. Jonathan told her that was over. He went out to the car and began bringing in the grocery.

After he had brought everything in Jonathan helped put away the grocery. Although Lucy enjoyed this closeness it felt strange. For so many years she had been alone................................

Several months passed and the family was getting to know each other. Raymond started coming over again. He and Jonathan would have their man's night. Lucy didn't know that Jonathan had as many friends as he did. Sometimes his pilot friends brought their wives and girlfriends with them. On those occasions she enjoyed the women's company. She liked Antela and Mark. They were a nice couple. She also enjoyed Pamela and Mitchell and Julie and James, but felt out of place because most of them knew each other through work and had jobs in common. Lucy felt bad sometimes because she didn't have any friends. Not that she kept in touch with Ruth or the others, but every so often when Jonathan had his friends over she felt lonely.

Lucy often thought of her friend Ruth. She wondered how she was doing. Lucy thought of Constance. She wondered if she was still following behind Paul. Jonathan interrupted her thoughts. He came up from behind her. Jonathan placed his arms around her waist and kissed Lucy on the back of her neck.

"What you grew tired of your friends?"

"No. I missed you. Oh by the way we ran out of food."

"I'll fix something."

"You don't have to do that. I can put something together."

They heard Joann crying.

"I guess you will have to fix something now."

She kissed Jonathan on the lips. She went into the refrigerator and got a bottle. Lucy warmed up the milk and headed upstairs. When Lucy got up to Joann's room she was standing holding onto the bars of the crib crying. Lucy talked to her telling Joann not to cry. Lucy picked her up. She sat down in the rocker. Lucy talked to Joann as she fed her...............

Jonathan put some food together. He then went down to the basement. Lucy gave Joann a bath and got her ready for bed. She stayed in her room until Joann had fallen asleep.....

After leaving Joann's room Lucy went to her bedroom and went to bed..........................

Jonathan came up hours later. He was tired and had drank more than his usual. Jonathan climbed into bed fully dressed. He fell asleep.

Shortly after he began to dream:

Jonathan was in the hospital. He was running a high temperature. He was very ill and his injuries were life threatening. Jonathan moaned as he did in the hospital. He called out Lucy's name. Jonathan tossed and turned..............

After some time Lucy awakened. She looked over at Jonathan. She realized that Jonathan was having a nightmare. She smoothed her hand over his chest. Lucy called out Jonathan's name and then gently shook him. After several attempts Jonathan awakened. He just stared at Lucy. Lucy called his name again. Lucy could tell that he didn't know where he was.

"Jonathan. Baby, are you alright? Jonathan."

Jonathan looked at her, continuing to stare at Lucy. He took her into his arms.

"Lucy is it really you?"

"Yes. What's wrong?"

"I was having a dream of when I was in the hospital. I'm sorry. I disturbed you."

"Don't be sorry. Jonathan you never told me about what happened."

"It's kind of foggy. I never had nightmares before now. I guest when I was in the Caribbean I was too busy trying to remember you."

"Do you mind talking about it? I mean maybe it'll help."

Jonathan laid back. He held his arms out to Lucy. She went into them and laid her head on his chest. Jonathan caressed her shoulder.

"I guest I should start at the beginning. The night I flew out the crew and I prepared the plane. We got on our way. We were in the air for about forty-five minutes and then the plane started experiencing trouble with the engine. I turned the plane around. It shook fiercely as if it was coming apart. It actually did. I tried to locate a place close to land. I alerted the flight crew and began preparing an emergency landing. I did the best I could, but the plane came apart. When it went down it split in two and I was thrown away from the others. When I was found it had been a few days and I was running a high fever. I had several broken bones. When I awakened the nurse told me that I had been unconscious for two weeks."

"The nurse?"

"Yes, it was her."

"Was she...I'm sorry."

"She was attractive, but not as beautiful as you."

"Stop."

"It's true. You are the most beautiful woman I've ever seen. Once I met you I have never had eyes for anyone else. She was kind. Her name was Sally. She took good care of your husband. Where was I? I know. When I awakened Sally ran to get the doctor. He came in with a broad smile and said that they thought they were loosing me a few times, but I kept calling Lovely Lucy. He asked me who you were. I'm sorry, I didn't know. Your name came to my mind constantly. It was so frustrating not knowing who you were or even myself."

"How long were you in the hospital?"

Jonathan smiled and then kissed Lucy on the forehead.

"Sweet heart I was in the hospital for several years. I couldn't remember who I was, couldn't walk and couldn't begin to try because my ribs were cracked. I was told that I might never walk again. I couldn't accept that. I had to lay there wrapped up until my ribs healed. The hospital was located in a poor area. They didn't have the advanced equipment that they have in the states. Once my ribs were healed I told the doctor that I wanted to try to walk. The doctor didn't give me much encouragement, because there was so much damage that he didn't believe that my legs would heal enough and work again. I was determined to prove them wrong. When I was finally released the nurse, Sally offered her place. I thought it nice and didn't think that she wanted more than to give me a place to stay, since I still had no memory. I stayed there a while with her taking me to therapy and helping me with my excercises in between therapy."

"You never suspected that she was into you?"

"Not for a while. One night after living there a year she asked if I was lonely."

"I told her that I didn't have time for anything accept regaining my memory and returning to you."

"What did she say?" "She said that she would be patient. Sally often asked how long was I going to wait. I told her as long as I had to. I told her that I couldn't start a new life in good conscious." Jonathan took his hand and placed it under Lucy's chin and lifted her head. "You see I could never forget you and believe me I will never dishonor you. I have to thank you for staying with me and taking in Joann. You are an exceptional woman and I'll love you forever."

"Jonathan do you know how much I love you?"

"How much?"

Lucy kissed him with passion that neither had ever experienced. Jonathan held her tight and the two were lost.......

A month went by. Lucy went to get the mail. She saw a notice from an attorney. Lucy opened it. As she opened it Lucy wondered why she was receiving a notice from an attorney. She slid the notice open. Lucy took the letter out of the envelope. She began reading it. Lucy's heart dropped. She felt sick. Lucy had to sit down. She made her way to the chair in the hall. Lucy couldn't believe what she had read. She sat there staring at it…………………..…..

The front door opened. Lucy did not hear it. Lucy looked up when she felt something on her shoulders.

"Are you alright?"

"Lucy couldn't speak. She handed Jonathan the letter. He read it and then bent down in front of her. Lucy knowing that it was painful told him to stand up. He told her that he was alright. Lucy stood, took his hand and led him into the den. They sat next to each other. Jonathan asked if she was considering answering the letter. At first she was quiet and then said that she thought it was behind her. Jonathan tried to comfort her by saying that she didn't have to answer it right now. Lucy layed her head on his chest. Jonathan held Lucy wishing that he could take away her pain……………..……

Jonathan noticed the difference in Lucy. She went about her day doing what she normally did, but it was mechanical. He felt she had lost something. Jonathan tried to console her, but nothing worked. He held her at night and tried to get her to talk out her feelings, but she denied anything was wrong……………………………..

Two months went by. Lucy had not responded to the letter. A second letter came. This time it was more personal. Included in the letter were names of Paul and Constance's victims, or what the letter called survivors. They all had answered the letter.

When Jonathan returned home from picking up the twins from school they found Lucy sitting at the kitchen table. She tried to appear in good spirits, but Jonathan saw it in her eyes that something was wrong. He told the children to go up to their rooms to do their homework.

When the children were upstairs Jonathan sat down beside Lucy. He took the letter from her hands and read it. After reading it Jonathan placed his arms around her and she went into them. She held onto him in desperation. Jonathan held her and caressed her back. Lucy finally gained composure and took her arms from around him. He slowly moved back. Jonathan looked at her. He asked if she was alright. Lucy was honest and said no. She stood up and said that she had to cook dinner. Jonathan told her that they could order something. Lucy told Jonathan that she had to keep busy. She kissed him lightly on the lips and then walked out of the room. Jonathan followed closely.

Jonathan sat at the kitchen table and watched as Lucy seemingly in a trance prepared dinner..

At dinner the children noticed that she was quiet. Joanna questioned her about it. Jonathan answered for Lucy by saying that she was just tired. Lucy tried to act up beat so the children would not be alarmed. She looked at her daughters and thought of the second letter that was sent. Lucy thought of the ages of some of the girls. Although none of them were younger than Joanna some of them weren't much older. She thought of how the youngest was sixteen years old. Lucy thought how awful that must have been for her....

When dinner was over J.J. walked over to Lucy. He bent down, kissed Lucy and then told her that he loved her. Joanna followed suit. The two went up to their rooms. Jonathan cleaned Joann up and took her over to Lucy. Joann kissed Lucy. Jonathan took Joann up to her room. He got her ready for bed and then put her in the crib. Jonathan bent down and kissed her. He said good night and then went back downstairs. Jonathan went into the kitchen. He began helping Lucy clear the leftovers. They stood side by side. She washed the dishes and he dried them.

When they were finished cleaning the dishes Jonathan and Lucy went upstairs together. They checked the children on the way to their room.

When they were in their bedroom Jonathan and Lucy prepared themselves for bed. He held her against him. As they lay in bed Jonathan questioned Lucy about her thoughts of answering the attorney. Lucy fought back tears. She couldn't hold back her secret any longer. Lucy confessed to Jonathan how her body had reacted to Paul's assault. She told him that it acted as if he had been a lover and she had wanted him to do the things that he did to her. Jonathan was quiet for a while. She could feel his body tense. Lucy felt guilty and told Jonathan as much, explaining that was one of the reasons that she didn't want to testify. Jonathan didn't speak. He held Lucy more firmly. She began crying and apologizing. Jonathan caressed her hair and then kissed it. He kissed her eyelids and then told her to look at him. Lucy was hesitant. She felt as if she had betrayed him. Lucy was afraid of what she would see in his eyes. Jonathan repeated himself. Lucy finally looked up. She was surprised at what she saw in his eyes. All she saw in Jonathan's eyes was love and compassion. She asked how could he look at her like that. Jonathan kissed her passionately. He then stopped and looked at her again. Jonathan placed his hand under her chin.

"There is no reason for you to apologize. You didn't do anything wrong." Lucy looked away. Jonathan turned her face back to his. "Beautiful you are a survivor. What that animal did to you and those women was cruel." Lucy saw his eyes change to anger. "He tried to take that special part of you, but he couldn't.""

"But…"

"But nothing. I love you. I see you the same way I did from the very first time that I met you."

Lucy laid in Jonathan's arms. He held her until she fell asleep….

The next morning Lucy reluctantly got up. She went down to the kitchen and began cooking breakfast. She then went back upstairs and knocked on J.J. and Joanna's door. She told them to get up. Lucy walked down the hallway and opened the door to Joann's room. Joann was still asleep. Lucy looked at her. She was getting big. Joann was going on two years old. Lucy walked over to her and kissed Joann. Joann woke up and smiled. She wrapped her arms around Lucy's neck and said, "Good morning momma." Lucy smiled. As Lucy picked Joann up she wondered if her biological mother ever had second thoughts. She wondered if she ever thought or wondered about Joann.

Lucy carried Joann down to the kitchen so she could check on breakfast. She placed Joann in her high chair. Lucy set the table. The twins came downstairs and sat at the table. Lucy fixed their plates. She sat down and ate a small amount. She was finished before the twins. She fixed Jonathan a plate and then washed the dishes. When the twins were finished eating Lucy told them to go out to the car. Lucy picked Joann up and carried her up to her bedroom. She called out to Jonathan. He opened his eyes. Joann called out daddy. Jonathan sat up. Lucy carried Joann over to Jonathan. She went to put Joann down. Joann held her around her neck and began to cry. Lucy told her that she would be right back. Jonathan took Joann from Lucy and began talking to her. Joann calmed down. Lucy kissed her and said she would be right back. Lucy hurried down the hallway and down the stairs. She left the house and got into the car. Lucy drove the twins to school.

When she arrived in front of the school Lucy parked the car. The twins kissed her and hurried out of the car and into the school.

Lucy sat out there a few minutes. She closed her eyes and prayed. Lucy recalled the letter from the law office. She remembered the women names and ages. Lucy couldn't believe Paul was so messed up in the head. She opened her eyes and drove home.................

When she arrived back home Lucy parked the car and went inside of the house. She looked around the house for Jonathan. She found him in the bedroom asleep. When she stepped into the room Jonathan awakened. He sat up and held his hand out to her. Lucy walked over to him. She took his hand. Jonathan pulled her to him. He held Lucy and caressed her hair. After a while Lucy drifted off to sleep. Jonathan held her as firmly as he could to give comfort. Jonathan wondered how he could help her get through what she was going through.......................

When Lucy awakened she tried to ease out of his arms. He held her tighter and asked where she was going. Lucy told him that she was going downstairs to get the letter from the attorney's office. Lucy confided that she was going to speak with the attorney. Jonathan looked at Lucy and asked if she was sure. Lucy placed her head on his chest. She explained that she had to help the attorney put Paul away and then added Constance. Jonathan rubbed her back. Lucy got up.

On her way down the hall she checked on Joann. Joann was still asleep. Lucy continued down the hall and then went downstairs.

When she got downstairs Lucy picked up the letter from the attorney and then read it again. She walked to the phone and dialed the law office. The phone rang three times. Just as she was about to hang up the phone she heard a woman's voice say hello. Lucy placed the phone back to her ear. Lucy said hello and then proceeded to tell the woman who she was and the reason for her call. The woman seemed excited to hear from her. She told Lucy to hold on. Lucy waited a few minutes and then the woman returned to the phone. She told Lucy that she was being transferred to Mr. Lewis, Esq.

When the line was transferred the attorney spoke and than introduced himself. He went over the particulars of the case and then thanked Lucy for calling. He asked if they could meet. Lucy was hesitant and then asked if she could bring her husband. The attorney told her it would be fine. They scheduled a date and then hung up.

Lucy hung up the phone, but kept her hand on the receiver a few minutes. She stayed in that position as if frozen in time. Lucy jumped when she felt a hand on her shoulder. Jonathan apologized for starling her. He looked at her. Seeing the expression on Lucy's face Jonathan placed his arms around her. She went into them. Lucy placed her head on his shoulder. They didn't say anything. The two remained frozen in that position for a while...

After some time had passed Jonathan whispered in Lucy's ear, asking if she was sure about going forward with seeing the attorney. Without looking up Lucy shook her head yes. She could not speak. Her throat was chocked up, not wanting to show how emotional she was……..

Finally she looked up at Jonathan with glassy eyes and managed to say that this was something that she had to do. Jonathan pulled her to him again………………

Several days later Jonathan accompanied Lucy to the attorney's office. She decided at the last minute not to have Jonathan go in for the interview. He stayed in another room with Joann. The attorney thanked Lucy for coming forward. Lucy was curious. She asked how did he get her name and information. The attorney told her that in order for Constance to get a lighter sentence she had to provide names and addresses of all the females that she had given to Paul. Lucy sat a few minutes trying to compose herself.

As she told her ordeal the secretary took everything down. Some of the time Lucy noticed the secretary look at her. Lucy wondered what the secretary thought of her. She wondered if Mr. Lewis thought she could have done something to stop Paul from doing the things that he had done. She felt humiliated, having to tell the details. When she was done Mr. Lewis thanked her. Lucy asked if he could submit her statement rather than she go to court. The attorney told her it was possible. Lucy asked if they were done. The attorney said that they were. He stood up and held his hand out. Lucy shook it. The attorney thanked Lucy for coming in. The secretary escorted her out.

She joined Jonathan. The couple left the office. It was time to pick up the twins so Jonathan drove to pick them up. As Jonathan drove Lucy filled him in on some of the information that the attorney had shared with her. Jonathan was happy that she didn't have to testify. The attorney informed Lucy that he was collecting information on Paul's victims. He also informed her that he would only need a few to actually testify. The attorney stated that he had enough women to testify. He said that he would use her information along with others to add to his evidence…..

A month later Lucy tried to get on with her life. She threw a birthday party for Joann. She was now a year older. Lucy watched this beautiful little girl play with her big brother and sister. She knew nothing about another life. She was smart and looked so much like her father. It didn't appear that Lucy wasn't her biological mother. Joann ran over to Lucy yelling mommy, breaking her concentration. Lucy looked down. She held her arms out and picked Joann up. Joann showed Lucy a toy that had been given to her. Lucy smiled as she looked at the toy and this little girl who knew no other mother than her. She hugged Joann. Joann excitedly showed her the toy and then ran off to play.

Jonathan walked up to Lucy and placed his arms around her. He held her from behind. Jonathan then said thank you. She knew what he meant.

"She is beautiful."

They watched on as the children played………………......

Sally sat on her porch looking out over the ocean. She wondered what Jonathan was doing. She wondered if his wife had waited for him and had she accepted their child. Sally then resolved that if she hadn't he would have returned to her.

"Sweet heart what are you in deep thought about?"

"I was just thinking about a past life."

"Have you grown tired of us?"

She looked down at her child and then at her husband.

"No I have not grown tired."

"I didn't mean to be gone away so long. I will never leave you again."

"I'm happy you returned. Twelve years was a long time, but I managed to survive."

"I know, but you matured. We were very young when we married. I had to find myself. I had to grow up. There's something different about you."

"Yes, but I was so lonely. Being alone changed me."

"Well you'll never be alone again. Your husband is back and I'll never leave you again."

Sally laid her head on her husband's chest. She thought of Jonathan and mourned her lost..............................

"Please stand for the Honorable James Jones, Presiding Judge."

"You may be seated."

"Prosecutor present your case."

"Your honor we're here today because of the unspeakable criminal acts this man and I use man lightly, raped twenty-five females that we know of. He is on trial for twenty-five counts to each following charges of aggravated rape, attempted murder and sexual assault. Mr. Paul Miles is more dangerous than most sexual predators. He was able to use another woman, a woman who believed she was his girlfriend, a Miss Constance Graves to gain entry into the female's homes. Miss Constance knew each woman who was either a friend to her or their parents. Miss Graves will be one of the witnesses that the state will call to the stand. The state will prove that none of these women consented or were willing participants in these sexual acts and many of the women had to receive medical attention involving fractures, multiple broken bones, stitches to private parts where Mr. Miles rip rectums and tore vaginas because of the barbaric assault. I would also like to add that many of the women were given venereal diseases and are still undergoing medical care to check for HIV and AIDS. While Mr. Miles does not have the AIDS virus because of what we know of this virus and Mr. Miles the health department would like to keep close eye on all involved. The state is asking that Mr. Miles receive a sentence of no less than twenty-five years for each woman known. Thank you."

"Defense."

"Your honor my client is innocent of all charges. My client admits to having sexual relations with these women named in this case, but maintains that it was consensual. He further maintains that these women were of the aggressive sort and the nature of their relationship were to act out scenes that the women pursued. The defense maintains innocence. Thank you."

"Prosecution present."

"I call my first witness Rebecca Gordon."

Rebecca stood and walked up to the witness seat. She was sworn in.

"Please state your name for the courts."

"Rebecca Gordon."

"What is your age?"

"Seventeen."

"Miss Gordon I know this is difficult for you, but can you point out the man and I use this loosely that raped you."

Rebecca pointed to Paul. He looked directly at her without any expression. Rebecca quickly turned away.

"Miss Gordon can you tell this court what happened on the night of October 1st at approximately 4:30 p.m." Tears filled up in Rebecca's eyes. She looked at the prosecutor. Rebecca cleared her voice. "Take your time."

"On October 1st my parents were away. They asked Constance to keep an eye on the house. That evening I had just gotten home from school. I still had my uniform on."

"Uniform?"

"Yes. I attend private school and we have to wear uniforms. I had just gotten in. The doorbell rang. I went to answer it. Constance was there. I opened the door and then went to my room."

"Do you usually just open the door and leave?"

"Constance is one of my mother's best friends. She watched me grow up. She use to baby sit me."

"So you trusted her?"

"Yes."

"What happened after you went into your room?"

"Constance came in. She asked me if I ever had sex." Rebecca looked down.

"I'm sorry but I have to ask. What did you tell her?"

"That I never."

"So you're a virgin?"

Tears ran down her cheeks.

"Objection."

"Over Ruled."

"Yes. I was." Rebecca wiped the water from her face.

"Take your time."

"He came into my room."

"Who Mr. Miles?"

"Leading the witness."

"Careful."

"Who came into your room?"

"Mr. Miles. He came into my room. Constance told me not to be afraid. She said your first time you're usually clumsy, so she wanted Paul to show me how to be good in bed. I told her that I didn't want to, that I wanted to wait. She said that Paul could show me some good moves, where the guy would never leave me. I told her they should leave." Tears build up in Rebecca's eyes again. She tried to wipe them away, but it was useless. "He came close to me. I moved back. Constance was behind me. She grabbed my arms." Rebecca's voice shook. "I couldn't get away. Constance put handcuffs on my wrist. She moved me to my desk chair. She tied a rope around my arms and to the chair. I cried out and then she placed duck-tape across my mouth." Rebecca's hand trembled as she wiped more tears from her eyes and placed them to her lips. "She pulled my blouse open and then my underwear down. Then she left him in the room with me alone."

"I know it's difficult, but the court needs to hear what he did to you."

"He did things."

"What things?"

"He talked and said it felt good." Rebecca told the courts all the intimate details. "I tried to tell him not to do this. He continued to say it was feeling good. Each time he finished he washed me. He said he didn't want me to get an infection. He sent Constance to get cream to put on me because he kept doing stuff. For two days Mr. Miles did different things to me, all the while telling me it will help me in the future with men. He said he was teaching me what men wanted their women to do in bed. For two days every two hours, all night he did things to me. I was in so much pain. He kept telling me to relax, but I couldn't, I had never had sex before. He wouldn't stop having sex. He put ointment, but it didn't help. Constance came in after the first day and gave me a power drink saying I had to keep my strength up. She put a hold just large enough to place a straw in my mouth so I could drink it. I tried to drink it but I ended up throwing it up.

Late the next day she untied me from the chair, but left on the handcuffs. Mr. Miles picked me up, saying this is how your husband will carry you on your wedding night. Once I was on the bed Mr. Miles said, "Now for the Good Stuff." Rebecca looked down. When she had gotten her composure Rebecca continued. She looked at he judge with tear-filled eyes, face socked, and "I don't understand why he did this to me. I didn't come onto him and I didn't know him until Constance brought him to my house. After the second day He let me rest for three hours and then started up again until late that night. After the two days Constance came back into the room and then they untied me and took the handcuffs off. He kissed me and said that I was good."

"What happened next?"

"My mother came home. She came into my room and saw me balled up crying. She asked if I was sick. My mother pulled back the covers and saw blood. She asked me what happened. I couldn't get it out. She figured something bad had happened and took me to the hospital. I told her that I needed to take a shower. She told me that she was sorry, but I had to go to the hospital the way that I was."

"What happened then?"

"My mother took me to the hospital. They gave me that pill. You know the one that make sure you won't have a baby. I was sore for a long time and then they called my mother and said I needed to go to the doctor to get a shot."

"A shot for what?"

"Ghonarea."

"He didn't use a condom?"

"No. He said that it felt better natural."

The court was quiet. The judge asked if he had any further questions. The judge asked if the defense wanted to cross-examine. The defense attorney stood and walked towards Rebecca.

"Rebecca you say that Mr. Miles forced you, but didn't you allow him to come into the house?"

"He came with Constance."

"But you let him in."

"Yes."

"When he came into your room did you ask him to leave?"

"Yes."

"How long did it take you?"

"I don't know."

"Objection. Relevance."

"I'm trying to establish the fact that she allowed this man into her room and had a sexual conversation knowing what he was after."

"I will allow, but watch it."

"So you say you asked him to leave, but not right away?"

"No, But…."

"You allowed him into your bedroom and you allowed Constance to handcuff you."

"Objection. Is he asking a question or telling the victim what happened to her?"

"Counselor I'm warming you."

"Miss Gordon you say that Constance is a family friend so you trusted her?"

"Yes."

"Did you know Mr. Miles?"

"No."

"No further questions."

"I would like to redirect."

"Proceed."

"Rebecca you saw Constance since she was a family friend, as someone who would not want to do you any harm."

"Yes."

"So when she came in and brought Mr. Miles you didn't take alarm."

"Yes."

"When Mr. Miles came into your room with Constance what did you do?"

"When she started getting personal I asked them to leave and then I tried to leave. That's when Constance put the handcuff around my wrist. Mr. Miles stood close watching. I was afraid to fight."

"Did you struggle at all?"

"Yes, but with the handcuffs behind me I couldn't do anything, but move my shoulders. Mr. Miles was standing in front of my door. He had closed it."

"Did you scream?"

"I couldn't."

"Why not?"

"They put tape on my mouth."

"Thank you."

"You may step down. Remember you're under oath in case the attorneys have additional questions."

Rebecca got up and walked to the prosecutor. He thanked her and she walked out of the courtroom.

"Counselor your next witness."

"I call Lauren Meadows."

Lauren came into the courtroom. She walked up to the stand. Lauren was sworn in.

"State your name for the court."

"Lauren Meadow."

"How old are you?"

"Eighteen."

"Could you tell this court why you're here?"

"I'm here because (Pointing to Paul), that man raped me."

"Can you tell this court what happened?"

"My mom's friend, Constance came over. She asked if my parents were home. I told her they had gone away for the weekend and wouldn't be home until Sunday. She asked me what was I doing that night. I told her that I didn't have any plans. Constance said that she was shocked that I was staying home on a Friday night. She asked me if I wanted some company. I told her no, that I was fine alone."

"What happened then?"

"Constance said that she had to use the bathroom. I told her where it was and then I went into my bedroom. I began to change my clothes. As I pulled my skirt off I turned around and Constance was standing in the door. She walked towards me. I thought she was coming over to say goodbye. As she kissed me on the cheek I felt something go around my arms. I looked down. It was a rope. I pulled my arms out and we struggled. She managed to get it around my arms again. I struggled, trying to get free. She got behind me and pulled me down onto the bed. She tied my hands to the bedpost. I asked her why was she doing this to me. She didn't say anything. She just walked out of the room. A few minutes later with me yelling let me go that man (Pointing at Paul again), came into my room. He closed the door. I asked him to please untie me. He smiled and told me to relax. He walked over to me and kissed me. He told me that he wasn't going to hurt me. He said all I had to do is enjoy the ride. I begged him not to. I told him that I was saving myself. He kissed me again and said thanks. He then began to kiss and touch my body. He asked me if it felt good. I pleaded for him to stop." Tears filled her eyes. "He did things to my body. I didn't want it."

"Can you be more specific? I'm sorry to ask you to relive this, but the court has to hear what you went through."

"He told me that he was getting me ready for the love of my life. He told me that although I may love someone else I would always think of how good he made me feel. He said that he would make my body call to him. I kept my mouth close, so he kissed me with a closed mouth. He licked my lips saying that I don't know what I was missing by not tasting him. I didn't want him to think that I was agreeing to what he wanted, so I continued to keep my mouth closed. He took off the rest of my clothes." Lauren looked down as she went into detail of what Paul did to her. Lauren began to cry.

"Do you want to stop?"

Lauren looked at the prosecutor. She wiped tears from her face. She looked directly at Paul.

"You may have made my body respond the way you think it supposed to, but it's still rape. I didn't consent. You took something I can never get back."

"Thank you. No further questions."

"Cross examine."

"I reserve."

"Counselor call your next witness."

"I call Jill Ramos."

Jill came into the courtroom. She took the stand and was sworn in.

"Please state your name and age."

"My name is Jill Ramos. I am twenty-five."

"What brought you here today?"

"I was raped."

"Is that man in this courtroom?"

"Yes. He's right there." Jill pointed to Paul.

"Tell this court how did you come to know Mr. Miles."

"I was at a club. Paul came up to me and asked to dance. We danced to a few songs. He bought me a few drinks. I started feeling out of it. He told me that he should take me home. I gave him my address because I needed to lay down. We got to my apartment. I thanked him for getting me home. He said he should make sure I get into bed. I gave him my keys. He opened the door. We went in. I said thank you and that he could leave my keys on the desk. I laid my head back. Just as I was drifting off I felt my hands go up. I didn't have any strength. I managed to see this woman. She was tying my hands to the bedpost. I asked what was she doing. She didn't speak. She left out. Then Paul came in. I asked what was going on. Paul told me to relax. He said that we were going to have some fun. I told him that I wasn't feeling well. He started removing my clothes. I asked him to please stop. He just told me to relax. Paul did things to me. Things I never would have done willingly. I cried because of some of the things he did hurt. He did some things that were painful. He told me if I relaxed it wouldn't hurt. He continued what he was doing. He did things to me for three days. Monday morning a woman cut the ropes and they left. At first I just laid there and cried. I was in so much pain. I had a difficult time walking. I looked at my sheets. There was blood on them. I thought of taking a shower and then I thought that this might be someone the police was looking for. I thought if he did this to me maybe there were others he had done the same thing to."

"Thank you. No further questions."

"Cross examine."

"Ms. Ramos you say that this man raped you?"

"Yes."

"Why is that?"

"I didn't give him permission to violate my body."

"Let's see, you were attracted to him. He's a handsome, charming man isn't he?"

"Yes, but."

"You gave him your address."

"Yes, but…"

"You gave him your key to your apartment."

"Yes."

"You didn't make sure he was out of your house before going to lay down did you? You left him in your apartment and went into your bedroom leaving a stranger in your house. You wanted to have sex with him."

"He was helping me."

"Yes and you wanted to return the favor."

"No. I was sick."

"Okay, as you told us of your terrible ordeal, there were times you looked at Mr. Miles and smiled. Why is that?"

"I don't know. I guess I'm nervous."

"Maybe because you enjoyed this. Maybe you liked Mr. Miles doing what he did. Maybe it wasn't rape."

Jill stood up.

"He did take advantage. I didn't say yes. I don't know why my body responded the way it did, but I didn't say yes."

"No further questions."

"Ms. Ramos you may step down. Thank you."

Jill stepped down from the stand. She walked pass the prosecutor and then looked over at Paul. She saw the same look on his face that he had when he was over her. She hated him for how he made her feel that weekend. She remembered when the counselor had gotten in touch with her. At first she had declined thinking how could she testify when she wasn't even sure it could be called rape. Sure she had not invited him in and sure she had not given consent to sex, but the way he had made her feel could it be considered rape. After several months the counselor convinced her that it was rape. Still Jill had her doubts. All she had ever known was that rape was painful and you would not feel good, but this was not the case for her, nor for many of the women she read about in this case. Jill composed herself and left out of the courtroom.

"Counselor call your next witness."

"Your honor I have twenty-two sworn affidavits from women who were raped by Mr. Miles. Two of which were injured."

"Objection. My client didn't cause those injuries, it was Constance Rivers who caused those injuries and besides my client has a right to face his accuser."

"I would like to submit the affidavits rather than use unnecessary court time and money."

"Permitted."

"I have one last witness."

"Call your witness."

Constance came into the courtroom. Constance walked up to the stand and was sworn in.

"Your honor Constance Rivers is a hostile witness."

"Well taken."

"Please state your name for the court."

"Constance Rivers."

"How did you come to know Mr. Miles?"

Constance looked over at Paul and smiled.

"I'm sorry." She turned and looked at the prosecutor. "I met Paul at a club. He was so handsome. He seemed lost. I approached him and he told me that he had just broken up with his girlfriend. I asked him if he wanted to talk about it. He said not really. I asked if he wanted me to go away. He said no. I saw pain in his eyes. I walked up to him and put my arms around him. He allowed me to. He placed his arms around me. Paul then asked if we could go somewhere alone. I asked if he had a car. He took me by the hand and we walked out of the club. A few yards from the club was Paul's car. It was away from the others in a dark secluded area. He opened the back door to his car. I didn't want to give him any ideas, but he seemed like he was hurting and for some reason I wanted to take that pain away. I got into the car. When he got in Paul placed his head on my chest. I placed my arms around his shoulders. He didn't cry. He was quite. After we had been there a few minutes Paul looked up at me and kissed me. It was so sensuous I allowed it. We kissed a few minutes and then he pulled me down under him. He was so strong. I told him that I wasn't ready to do anything. He looked at me and said that he just needed to be close to a warm body. He said that he just needed to feel a woman. I don't know why, but I wanted to be that woman." She looked at Paul. "I fell in love with him at that moment. I told him it would be alright if we kissed and he could touch me, but we couldn't go any further than that. He kissed me and I melted into his hands. He said he needed me. I told him that I couldn't. He kissed me again. He pulled my blouse open and squeezed my breast. Not really hard, but I knew he was losing control. I told him that he needed to control himself. He unzipped his pants. At first he moved on top of me. I thought maybe he could get satisfied that way. I decided if I moved with him he could relieve himself. He kissed my breast and held me with such strength. I wanted to give him what he wanted, but I had just met him. He then began to try to get in. I told him no. Please no. He said he had to. He said that he loved me and he had to make our love complete. I pleaded with him no." Constance looked at Paul. She had tears in her eyes. "He lost control. But it wasn't all bad he made my body melt under his touch."

"So you're saying that your first encounter with Mr. Miles he raped you."

She looked at the prosecutor. She seemed confused at his question. "Ms. Rivers do you need me to repeat the question?"

"I don't know what you mean."

"Paul Miles forced you to have sex with him."

"I don't know if you'd call it that."

"Didn't you just say that you told him no?"

"Yes, but he needed me."

"So you don't call being forced to have sex with someone who you clearly and repeatedly said no to is rape?"

"It wasn't like that. Paul made me feel good. He made me feel wanted."

"How did it make you feel he having sex with all of those women and asking you to assist?"

Constance looked down. Then she looked at the prosecutor.

"Paul has a sexual disorder."

"What might that be?"

"He has a sickness. He has to have sex more than others and when he gets like that he has to have it. I tried to do everything he asked, but I wasn't enough." She looked over at Paul. "I'm sorry. I couldn't be enough."

"So you're telling this court that Paul Miles has a sexual disorder?"

"Yes. He can't control it."

"So what you're saying is that it's okay for him to force himself on women because he has this disease?"

Constance lowered her head.

"No." Tears filled her eyes."

"Were you aware that he had a venereal disease?"

"Yes, but he said that he took care of it."

"Were you with him every encounter?"

"I didn't stay in the room."

"So you stayed in another room for how long he assaulted these women?"

"Yes."

"Why?"

"I love Paul. I didn't want to see him having sex with any other woman."

"But you brought him to them."

"Yes."

"Why?"

"I love Paul. I couldn't satisfy him. I couldn't give him everything he wanted. I tried and he sometimes went to prostitutes, but it was too costly. That's where he contracted the disease. He didn't know at first. He told me as soon as he realized it. I got checked and cured. He went too and got a shot. Taking him to these women who I knew were either pure or was not out in the street it was the least that I could do to get him someone who could relieve him even if it was only for a little while."

"You didn't see anything wrong with this?"

"I was trying to help."

"Who restrained the women?"

"I did. It was so they wouldn't hurt themselves or Paul."

"How is that?"

"They may have fought and someone may have gotten injured. I washed them to keep them from getting an infection. I also tried to feed them so they would keep up their strength. Paul requires a lot, so sex is very exhausting. He always made sure that he satisfied the women. I sometimes heard them. He is gentle and so giving of himself. He's not selfish."

"No further questions."

"Defense."

"Ms. Rivers you said that the women all tend to enjoy their time with Mr. Miles."

"Yes."

"No further questions."

"Prosecution would like to question Ms. Rivers again."

"Proceed."

"Did any of these women invite Mr. Miles into their home?"

"No."

"No further questions."

"Miss Rivers you may step down."

Constance stood up. She left the stand. As she walked pass Paul she looked at him. She was relieve when he did not look angry.

"Counselor any further witness?"

"Prosecutor rest."

"Defense."

"I call Paul Miles to the stand."

Paul stood. He walked up to the stand. Paul was sworn in."

"Mr. Miles please state your name for the courts."

"Paul Miles."

"Paul Miles did you rape any of these women?"

"No."

"Did you have sexual intercourse with any of the women named in the complaint?"

"I met each one of those women. We had a good time, exchanged some body fluids and enjoyed it while doing so."

"Did any of these women protest?"

"That's the game. Women are taught to say no. I understand that. My job is to persuade them that it's a pleasure in going with the flow. If you ask any of these women who have been solicited in teaming up with the prosecutor they will tell you that they felt pleasure with every touch."

"Mr. Miles is there any truth that you have a medical condition?"

"I don't know if it's a medical condition, but I think that I am a sex addict."

"Have you ever been treated for this disorder?"

"No."

"How do you know you suffer from this condition?"

"I looked it up."

"Would you like help?"

"Yes."

"No further questions."

"Cross examine."

"Mr. Miles you say that you have this sexual disorder."

"I said I'm addicted to sex."

"Why haven't you ever gone to the doctor for this?"

"I didn't know something was wrong until just resent."

"So you had a revelation."

"Objection."

"Nothing further."

"Defense."

"Defense rest."

"Closing arguments."

"The prosecution ask the courts to rule guilty of twenty-five counts of 1st degree rape, aggravated assault, aggravated sexual assault, and attempted murder because Mr. Miles knowingly transmitted a venereal disease to these women and unlawful entry."

"Defense."

"In light of the new information provided about my client we ask that 1st degree rape be thrown out, aggravated assault, attempted murder and unlawful entry."

"Thank you counselors. Case is adjourned until December 15th."

Everyone exited the courtroom....

"Are we going to start getting the children Christmas gifts tomorrow?"

"Sure. You know this will be our second Christmas together."

"Yes I know. It all seems so strange. We've been married for thirteen years now and everything is still new for us. I missed so much. The twins are almost grown and I know very little about them. They are good kids. You did a really good job raising them."

"I've tried to do my best. I missed you so much. They still have many years to grow up. I'm grateful that you're here now. These are the hardest years they say, raising teenagers. You know we need someone to stay with them while we go shopping."

"How about Raymond?"

"He has stayed here on occasion. Do you think he'll be available tomorrow?"

"I'll call and ask."

Jonathan went up to their bedroom. He dialed Raymond's cell. Raymond answered on the second ring. The two men talked a while and then Jonathan asked Raymond if he was available. Raymond told Jonathan that he was spending the day with his new lady. Raymond told him that maybe they could come over for a little while. Jonathan thanked him, but declined on his offer. Lucy came upstairs. Jonathan informed her of his conversation. Lucy called an agency. She explained that she had used the agency before. The next morning the doorbell rang early. Lucy was dressed. She went down to answer the door. She was pleasantly surprised when she opened the door and the woman had watched the children before. Lucy asked her in. She talked with the woman a few minutes and then excused herself. Lucy went up to her bedroom and woke Jonathan up. After he woke up Lucy returned downstairs. She told the sitter that there was a toddler. Lucy told the sitter what to feed the baby and older children.

Jonathan came downstairs. Lucy introduced them and then she and Jonathan left. Lucy confided that the sitter had watched the children before. He was relieved that at least the twins knew her. As they drove to the toy store Lucy told Jonathan what the children wanted for Christmas.....

Joann woke up. She called out mommy. After a few minutes the sitter came into the room. Joann cried out mommy. Joanna awakened. She got up and went into Joann's room. She didn't recognize the sitter at first. Joanna asked the sitter who she was and where were her parents. The sitter explained who she was and that their parents had to go out for a little while. Joann continued to cry for her mother. She reached her arms out to Joanna. Joanna told the sitter that she'd take care of her. The sitter ran bath water and assisted Joanna in giving Joann a bath. When they were finished bathing Joann the sitter helped lift her out of the tub. Joann clung to her sister. Joanna dressed her and they went downstairs. The sitter fixed Joann's food. Joann sat next to Joanna while she ate.

A half hour later J.J. walked into the kitchen. He saw the sitter. He spoke and then asked where his parents were. Joanna told him. Joann reached for him. J.J. walked over to her and began playing with her. Joanna took this as a way to get away. She told J.J. to stay with her while she got dressed. As she was walking out of the kitchen Joanna asked if their parents were going to return. J.J. told her that their parents would be back. J.J. took Joann out of her high chair and carried her to the den. He sat down and played with her. Joanna came into the room. J.J. placed his arm around her shoulders. He said, "They're coming back." The sitter came into the room. She turned on the television. The sitter asked if there were anything they would like to watch. Joanna told her what Joann liked. The sitter turned to the channel. Joann's attention was directed to the television. The other children set quiet.........................

For two hours the children sat quietly and close together while watching cartoons on the television....................

At 12:00 the sitter got up and prepared sandwiches for the children. Just as they were about to eat the front door opened. The children heard it and with baby in her arms Joanna ran to the door, with J.J. right behind them. When they saw their parents the children ran up to Lucy and Jonathan and hugged them.

"What's this?"

"We miss you mom."

"She thought you weren't coming back."

"Where did you go?"

Lucy kneeled down. She held Joanna's face in her hands.

"Why would you think me and daddy would leave you?" Joanna looked down. "We love you. We would never leave you."

"Dad left."

"He didn't mean to."

Jonathan walked over to Joanna and picked her up.

"Daddy loves you. Sweetheart if I could have remembered I would have been back sooner, but I was injured. I tried to remember everyday. As soon as I remembered I came home as soon as I could. That's why I retired early. I wanted to make sure I was never apart from you again."

Joanna hugged him. J.J. surprised them. He walked over to his father and hugged him around his waist. Jonathan put his arm around J.J.

The sitter came into the room. Lucy noticed her. She walked into the foyer. Lucy paid the sitter and thanked her. The sitter said bye to the children and then left....................

That night Lucy heated up leftovers. They sat for hours at the kitchen table with Lucy and Jonathan reassuring the children of their love and devotion to them....................

Two weeks before Christmas the phone rang. Lucy was home alone. Jonathan had taken the children Christmas shopping. Lucy picked up the phone.

"Hello."

"Hi. Remember me?"

"Yes. Hi Ruth. How are you?"

"I'm fine. I heard Jonathan returned."

"Yes."

"I know it's been a long time. I didn't call because I got the impression that you didn't want to talk to me anymore."

"It wasn't you."

"I know. I'm still friends with Constance. She needs someone and I'm all she has now. Her family has turned their backs on her. I know she did some really bad things, but we all have to ask forgiveness for something. I didn't call to tell you that. I was missing my friend."

"I miss you too."

"Can we get together sometimes?"

"I guess so."

"How are those daring twins?"

"They are fine. I have another little girl now."

"Really?"

"Yes. She's eighteen months now."

"Wow. I have been away a long time. Well I'm not going to keep you. It was good hearing your voice."

"Same here. Thanks for calling."

The two women hung up. Lucy sat down and thought of the phone call. She had missed her friend and their talks. Lucy thought about Constance. She wondered how she could have done this to her friends. Lucy stopped herself from thinking about the past. She walked into her living room and thought how beautiful the tree looked. She recalled how it seemed more exciting this year putting it up. She went into the hall closet and walked towards the back of it. She took out a few gifts that she had purchased for Jonathan. Lucy took them into the living room and wrapped them. She placed them under the tree.

As she was putting the wrapping paper up Lucy heard the phone ring. She ran to answer it. She picked up the receiver. The voice on the other end of the phone identified himself as the prosecutor James Brown. Lucy's heart quicken. She sat down. He asked if he was speaking to Lucy Mills. She confirmed that he was. He told Lucy that the courts had come back with a verdict of guilty for first-degree rape, on all twenty-five counts. They dismissed all the other charges and downgraded the aggravated assault to simple assault. The attorney went on to say that Paul would be going to a mental facility for sex offenders for ten years, paroled for ten years and monitored through intensive supervision for seven years. He stated that he would also have to place his name on the sex offender's registry. The prosecutor also gave Lucy Constance's outcome. He thanked Lucy for her help. She didn't feel like she was of much assistance, but accepted his gratitude. Lucy thanked the prosecutor. She then hung up the phone.

Lucy went into the kitchen. She began preparing dinner. Lucy thought of Constance's sentence. She had been sent to jail for two years. She was also given a five-year probation sentence. Lucy was startled when Jonathan came up from behind her. She jumped. Jonathan asked if she was alright. Lucy asked the whereabouts of the children. Jonathan told her that they were in the living room wrapping her gifts and he was instructed to keep her out of there. Lucy informed Jonathan of her phone call from Ruth and then of the attorney. He listened intently to what she told him. Jonathan took her hand and asked if she was alright. Lucy told him that she would be..........................

As the days got closer to Christmas the children became more excited. Lucy's mood had also improved. Christmas Eve the children went to bed early. Lucy and Jonathan took this time to share their gifts with each other. They were happy for this quiet moment. It was late when they went to bed. Lucy laid in Jonathan's arms, thinking how good it felt being in his arms. She closed her eyes and nestled her head in his chest. Lucy thanked God for her family and things finally feeling like it was getting normal. She drifted off to sleep.

What seemed like they had just gotten asleep was broken when the children including the baby ran into their room, screaming Merry Christmas.

The family went downstairs. Jonathan and Lucy watched as the children excitedly opened their gifts.

Lucy had never felt such warmth as she did at this moment. She finally felt complete..................